Hemorrhage

Robert Shepyer

Published by Rogue Phoenix Press, LLP
Copyright © 2020

ISBN: 978-1-62420-462-3

Credits
Cover Artist: Natasha Chomko
Editor: Sherry Derr-Wille

Part One

Chapter One

Man

The *image* is not enough. That's why at some point of my young life, I decided to trade my paintbrushes in for a typewriter and live for the *word*. In my paintings, I was able to take snapshots of worlds far beyond this one, but after staring into the eyes of the characters I breathed life into, I decided they deserved a history and future. No painting could capture the complexity of the stories I desired to create. A novel, though, can capture everything.

An image can capture the moment but so what? Cameras are everywhere now, immortalizing everything: the 'moment' loses value. You're told to seize it, to live in it, to never let it slip between your fingers, but now, we are seeing the snag of that mentality. Living in the moment leads to nothing but chaos, dysfunction, and selling your soul. Not for a moment did I ever live in one. I prefer to live simultaneously in the future and past. Any time but the present. Working for a goal, embittered by memories. This method of being is no cakewalk, though. I'm absolutely penniless, without an asset to my name spanning back four generations to the great Jewish erasure. The only inheritance that trickled down from the dead were gaggles of ghosts to haunt me. I harnessed those voices and turned them into characters, symbols, places and dreams. For this I am forever grateful. The gift of a visit from the dead is invaluable.

Hemorrhage

~ * ~

Lying in my bed, in my parent's modest Burbank apartment while on vacation from my second year of university, I would let the days spin out. Existing in a timeless void, sinking upward in the hourglass sands, waiting to be turned topsy-turvy to restart. I would conjure such poetic thoughts then let them fade into the abstract, forgetting everything. I would think of fifty poems and in between stanzas imagine how wonderful being a writer would be. Then maybe, if the universe was lucky, I'd write something down. I presumed the writer's life was the one for me. Slackering through the streets with cigarettes stuffed in the fold of my cranberry beanie, holding a bottle of cheap raspberry wine to take home. Recognized and mythologized by a solid few gripes and hipsters, staying in a studio half the size of a prison cell, I would write things that would reshape the world. Words and stories that could break the bondage of those oppressed by our prison-style culture. For language is the most impenetrable prison, second only to the body. I would bring evil out into the daylight for us to chase away into the gutters. These ambitions required two things: delusion and patience. Two things I had in such abundance I could grow fat, devouring them for sustenance. I had the delusion to think I could change the world, could set it free, save us all, and never die. I had the patience to sit in one chair, writing all day while the world outside passed the time finding love, getting rich, having children, and building their reputations. To me though, in a weird way, I was doing all this too, chittering away at my typewriter and sending out some low-frequency signal to the universe. Once that signal finally reached the celestial satellite's receiver, it would bounce back and hit the gospel-hungry ears of the people. Someday this routine will give me everything anyone could ask for, even though no one is asking for writers.

What gives writers access to truth? What makes me think that I know more than you when I haven't spent a goddamn day truly *living* in the world? I credit pain. Pain perverted my mind into the shape of a skeleton key that could open any doors in heaven's hall of knowledge, no matter how hidden, doubly locked, or reinforced they were. I had every channel and floodgate opened. Having dealt with pain, I had the tolerance to absorb the electrical flow all this information carried without letting it drive me crazy. For so long, I thought I needed love. I thought if I had a woman, I would be able to tackle any spiritual hurtle and glide to success, but I was wrong. Pain, not love, was all I ever needed to create and withstand anything.

~ * ~

After months spent forgetting everything I learned in my English courses, letting my reading list pile up to my nose, the time finally came to pick classes for the upcoming semester. Having finished all my meaningless course requirements, I was able to have my schedule solely consist of art. I would take playwriting, Russian literature, poetry, and painting. I looked forward to keeping my painting supplies in my room so my clothes could reek of turpentine fumes that would creep into my mouth while I slept to derange my imagination further.

"Benny, dinner is ready," my mother shouted from the living room.

"Coming, Ma," I barked back.

I swiveled around in my chair and left my computer to grab dinner. Mom was a pretty good cook. Though she would only make the same four recipes, these classics had no comparison in the culinary world. The thick, white fog of meatballs over rice rose up from the plate that awaited me at the dining room table, which was also the living room table. I slid into my seat and began cramming it into my mouth till it was gone in under two minutes.

"You must be really hungry, cooped up in your room all day. What can you be doing in there for so long anyway?"

"Writing."

"I've never heard writing that sounded like that. The noises I hear out of your room are so strange."

"I guess I get really animated."

With a worried look on her face, she set down the next course. Caesar salad, mashed potatoes, and a chicken drumstick covered in what looked like gravy but couldn't have been. Before I could finish the plate, my lightning-fast pace was put on pause by the thundering intrusion of my father coming home after a long day of work.

"Shouldn't you be out looking for a job?" my father asked, as he swooshed by, trying to reach the bathroom before he could soil himself. I knew he meant the question rhetorically because he left so quickly that he couldn't have expected a response. Not that I would've had one anyway, other than "work is for suckers." The sounds of the toilet flushing ushered my father back to the dining table with liquid lucidity. He took the seat beside me at the same moment as a plate was set under his nose.

"Did you write today?"

This was the very first time he had ever asked me this.

"No," I confessed.

"Why the hell not?"

"I guess I didn't have anything to say today."

He swallowed his mouthful of masticated meat and turned to me. Looking into my eyes he groaned, "*Bull*," then turned right back to his food.

I thought for half a second, excused myself from the table and headed back into my room to write.

Chapter Two

Woman

The dead can dance if you teach them. That is the art of puppetry, animating the dead. I don't know what it was about puppets that consumed me. Perhaps it was the fact so many of my close family members died when I was young and this was my way of bringing them back to life. In fact, I fashioned a few of my puppets after their old pictures, with skin tone painted in gray scale. These classic golden-age figures had a class and sophistication that was foreign to anyone still alive. All my puppets get a kiss goodnight before I put them to bed in their own magic cupboard. As an only child, my parents spoiled me. Still, no presents or clothes could've satisfied me as much as a lifelong, platonic companion, like a sibling. These puppets are family to me, brothers, sisters, aunts, uncles, grandparents, and children, all at once.

My destiny as a puppeteer was already decided but I still needed to pick a major that would roll off the tongue to inspire good conversation over drinks. I concentrated and finally settled on "Fine Art." I picked painting, drawing, and sculpture for my classes next semester.

To celebrate finally making this decision, I pulled out my golden cigarette case and retrieved a joint. I lit it by the open window, thinking my mother was asleep and wouldn't smell it. One whiff and she claimed she could feel the THC's weight in the air throughout every room of the house. After the first hit, I watched the smoke spiral, dance, and dissolve, letting it represent the fucks I give.

That's when Jinx skittered across my room from behind my favorite teddy bears and leaped onto my lap to cuddle. The long ash end of my joint fell off onto his fur but he shook it off into a cloud of bleak fibers. I petted Jinx roughly, how he loved it, until he purred himself into a luxurious goop. Discovered behind a Brooklyn special effects shop's dumpster, the curious critter crept up on me while I was diving for buried treasure in the trash. This sort of serendipity is constant in my life. It's as if I am flawlessly directing these moments from dreams into reality.

"I'll tell you a secret, Jinxy."

His eyes stayed low but his ears perked up, listening.

"I'm clairvoyant. I see things before they happen."

Truly. I saw my encounter with Jinx before it happened. I've seen my career in puppeteering. I've seen all the lovers I will ever have and I've seen this world end. The enormity of the bloodshed will only be dwarfed by the grandness of a silence older than time. The horrors of our undoing will be amoral and undeserved. If the Earth foolishly desires humanity's destruction as vengeance for all we've burdened it with, then the Earth must not mind that it will die right by our side. If anyone should be put on trial for the coming end, it should be nature itself. Nature permitted man from the very first cell. Humanity's design, destiny, and death were ingrained in that cell's mitochondria. Through observation, one can only deduce human behavior is inspired by the Earth's behavior and because nature has not regulated itself with law like mankind has, to nature nothing is forbidden. For example, the sin of breaking the Sabbath. If nature would abstain from growth for just one day of rest, rot, and attrition, perhaps it would be spared from divine wrath.

"Charlotte," my mother shouted from the other room.

"I thought you were sleeping."

"Who cares what I was doing? Are you smoking in your room again?"

"No."

"Then why do I feel it in the kitchen?"

"It's psychosomatic. It's all in your head."

"Come out here, let me smell you."

I stood up and Jinx jumped off my lap to continue dicking around my room. I floated over to my door and opened it to meet my mother in the hallway. I groaned and dropped my shoulders, dragging myself over to her in obvious defeat. Her nostrils flared once, and her eyes peered into sharp ovals.

"Liar. How many times do I have to tell you?"

"Sorry."

"No allowance for you tonight."

"But James is coming over."

"Have him pay for once. Better yet, stop buying pot and save your money."

"James is a struggling writer, *Mom*. He can't pay for two people's dinner."

"Get ice cream."

"He's thirty-five, *Mom*. He doesn't *eat* ice cream."

She laughed in my face. Not because the statement was ridiculous but because she knew someday, I'm going to look back on this and wonder how I could be stupid enough to fall for a guy like James, older than me but with less going for him.

"You know, one day you're going to look back at your life and say to yourself, *Mom was right*, I was wasting my time with that loser."

"I doubt it."

James was devilishly handsome. The right scars perfectly complementing every downward slash of his hair. Why should I regret dating a beautiful loser? I'm not looking for anyone to take care of me yet.

~ * ~

James arrived outside my house at eight twenty-one p.m. I told him I needed ten more minutes to get ready but I was only petting Jinx, watching the end of an episode of *Pee Wee's Playhouse* I'd already seen three times. Once finished, I crawled out of my sofa and speedily exited my house, giving James the impression I was hustling to his car. With deliberate shortness of breath, I hugged, kissed, and greeted my boyfriend.

"Hey babe, sorry about that," I said, half of me in his arms.

"No worries. Glad you made it."

His hands returned to his stick shift and he put the car into second to speed up my street. We spent the next few minutes debating what to eat and settled on In-N-Out burgers. Sitting around a red round table on a warm, L.A. summer night, we scarfed down our burgers in gloriously repugnant fashion. He ate a Double-Double and to one-up him, I ordered a Four-by-Four, which I finished in half the time it took him to eat his.

"No matter how much I eat, I never get fat."

"When your arteries finally clog at forty and you have a heart attack, at least the EMTs won't have trouble carrying your skinny body into the ambulance."

I laughed so hard I could feel vanilla shake seeping out of my nose.

"Dude, that is so messed up."

"Why? A heart attack isn't the worst way to die."

"Definitely not, I'm hoping for something a little more...*dramatic*."

"Dramatic how?"

"Being devoured by one thousand hummingbirds."

James smiled and laughed with his eyes fixed onto mine. This was his way of telling me I was great. That I was special. Not a typical girl. One he was supremely lucky to be with.

Chapter Three

Man

I once had a dorm mate but did everything in my power, short of violence, to force him out. After this Rudy character left, the dormitory service couldn't find a replacement willing to deal with my shit so they left me to my own devices. I am the scourge of this dormitory. Quiet and foreboding, I walk through the halls with a cloud of strangeness that catches every glance and diverts every conversation my presence interrupts.

The moment I returned after summer break, I unpacked my books, stacked them in the order they must be read and laid in bed to start. The first book was *The Kabbalah*, the Jewish book of mysticism. Theorizing this world is a broken vase and it is humanity's duty to return the broken pieces to its original form, I hoped reading this book would inspire a more biblical flare to my prose. Born and raised a conservative Jew, this university was my first truly secular and diverse experience. I was familiar with the Torah and Mishnah but the *Kabbalah* always seemed forbidden to children. As if you needed to know the previous texts like the back of your hand before you could be worthy of cracking it open.

One concept in the *Kabbalah* is the difference between men and women. Women are earthly, nurturing, tolerant, and patient. Men are cosmic, more philosophical and connected to the stars. After reading fifty pages, I got out of bed and went outside to get a closer look at the grass and trees, trying to understand women. Sap glazed bark on the life-giving totems. Angry, warped faces in the wood. The breeze, the trees, the animals, the sun, the sky, the clouds, the water, all these things speak to people. Writers truly listen. A girl walked up to me, smiling from ear to ear. She was the most beautiful girl in the world.

"Nice day out, isn't it?"

"I guess."

"Do you live in the dorms?"

"What else would I be doing out here?"

"I'm sorry, am I bothering you?"

"No…I just don't like small talk."

"Same. I hate small talk too."

"What do you see when you look at that tree?" I said and pointed at it.

"Bark. Leaves…"

"It's a cedar tree. The same kind of wood that was used to craft Noah's ark, the ark of the covenant, and Christ's cross."

"Interesting. You seem pretty brainy."

"*Me?* No," I joked sarcastically but she didn't catch my drift.

"Well, I have to get going. It was nice speaking to you."

"Adios."

My heart locked up as if it was being stuck with so many pins that I wouldn't dare speak in fear of lodging them in deeper. She nodded and awkwardly scurried away. Not that she was awkward. Every interaction I have with the opposite sex seems to end that way. I hung my head, so depressed. She must've mistaken me for someone more handsome and been rather disappointed when I turned around to greet her. She was so creeped out.

Chapter Four

Woman

My two best friends, Esa and Molly, who also just happen to be my roommates, pressured me into getting my first tattoo the other day. We got ink of the animal nicknames we call each other. I got a spider, Molly got a moose, and Esa got an elephant. These animals represented our personalities, with Esa being kind and wise, Molly being strong and feisty, and myself small and instinctually able to create beautiful art…plus the book, *Charlotte's Web*.

I suppose my size is the reason I've always wanted to marry a tall fellow, at least six feet two inches. I see it happening so it will. I don't see a name and or a face but still, I envision him protectively towering over me, our shadows melding together as one. I figure too, a tall husband means tall children, no matter my size.

Esa and Molly decorated their rooms much more flamboyantly than mine. Molly had her hunks hung up on the walls. Lead singers with crotch rockets and heroin-handsome nineties models were her fix.

Esa was a nerd. She filled her room with everything Japanese and superheroes galore. Me, I had a desk where I'd fashion wooden puppets and a trash bin beside it where I'd discard the shavings.

We were all in the living room, watching a romantic comedy and smoking weed from my bong. It was a beautiful piece of glass, one and a half feet of frosted perfection with a percolator and ice catcher to make the hits smooth as silk. Esa and Molly took their hits, each coughing up an obnoxious storm. When the piece came back to me, I hit it and held in the smoke until it started fuming out my nostrils like I were a dragon. No coughs or whimpers, I exhaled like a pro. Stoned as fuck, the romantic comedy felt far more romantic than funny, at least to our sappy trio.

We heard a knock at the door and quickly dried our eyes. Seeing as the other girls were far too high to speak, I volunteered to pull myself off the couch and trip some poor stranger out. On the other side of the door was an adorable and peevish blonde.

"Hey there, girls, I'm from the sorority Kappa Kappa...."

"Put a cap on it." I slammed the door in the recruiter's face before she could get out the last Greek letter.

We laughed so hard that we nearly burst into three piles of pink confetti. Esa and Molly covered me in kisses, reminding me they loved me to death. The three of us never end up drifting apart. We simply don't let it happen.

Chapter Five

Man

My first class of the semester was playwriting, taught by a Marxist and failed ventriloquist who began the class with a lecture on Dario Fo and Bertolt Brecht. We learned all it took to break the proletariat's chains was making art transcendent enough to rehumanize the oppressors. My first assignment was to write a five-page two-person play in a single setting of my choice. I already knew I'd set it in a dungeon.

Following playwriting was Russian literature. Russians, to me, are the best people at churning out brilliant and tortured novels. Mostly because their methods of torture were brilliant. Dostoevsky, the Czar of Russian writers, wrote books I perceived as essential in understanding the roles of good and evil in this world. The man nearly resolved the question of suffering.

My second to last class of the day, which would round out my English major requirements for the semester, was poetry. I took this class solely for the lecture on Arthur Rimbaud, the little gay demon teen who changed the fate of art with a rebellious attitude and visceral impression of Paris.

We'd get there eventually but before Rimbaud, we had to study Baudelaire. Before Baudelaire, we had to understand Byron. Byron rather bored me with the exception of one stanza of *Childe Harold* where he indicates the predictors of social decay. Predictors that numerous other iconic thinkers spoke of as well. Predictions happening now like the decay of language and the blurring of social boundaries.

My final class of the day was painting, located at a different end of the campus that forced me to walk through the sort of gatherings you'd see in Hieronymus Bosch paintings. Strange players moving in some kind of symbolic dance. When I arrived at the painting studio, I sat before an empty easel on a stool between two other empty stools in the foolish hope they wouldn't be taken. Dashing that hope, one overweight Asian boy took the seat to my right and a beautiful, short, pale-skinned girl took the seat to my left.

"Hey," she said, unforgettably.

Chapter Six

Woman

He was tall and looked like he hadn't gotten sun in months. His crooked skeleton hunched over his stool as if this position was what came naturally to him. I knew he was a writer at that moment, analyzing the shape of his spine weighed down by his skull.

"Hey," I said, figuring there was no way in hell he would've made the first move.

"Hi," he responded with a quiet and unprepared shyness.

"Haven't I seen you before? Did you take bio-lab last year?"

"I did."

"With who, Dr. Chi?"

"No, but I took Tai Chi."

"How was that?"

"Life changing until summer rolled around and I forgot everything."

That dark, charming earful pulled at my heartstrings but before I could even emote back, the professor demanded our attention at the front of the classroom.

"None of you are going to be the next Da Vinci, but don't get discouraged. You're not here to sell anything to the Met or even make the standout pieces in your portfolio. You're here to learn the basics of painting."

After a short lecture including a boastful slideshow of his work, the teacher introduced us to our utensils. Our first task was simply to prepare a canvas, pulling it over the wooden frame, stapling it in back, then lucidly coating it with gesso, getting hypnotized by the stuffy vapor.

"Have you ever painted before?" the boy asked me.

I turned to him and caught his eyes staring right at me.

"Yeah, a bit. I make puppets and paint their faces."

"Cool."

Those were all the words we'd share for the rest of the class until bidding each other farewell, at which point I learned his name was Ben and he learned mine was Charlotte.

On the walk back to my dorm, I got a text from James. Last week, he claimed he signed a major publishing contract and landed a three-book deal. However, I didn't see him living up his new wealth or spoiling me. James was neither a minimalist or cheap when he had money, so I figured he was lying to keep me attached to him while I was in school.

How was your first day, kiddo? he texted.

It was cool. Western Civilization seems boring. Art history too. Painting seems like it'll be relaxing.

I'm going to be interviewed by this big book magazine.

Which one?

Lit Lock.

Never heard of it.

He didn't text again until the evening and I didn't respond. I was already thinking about how to get Ben to go out with me. Back at my dorm, the girls and I decided to order Chinese food. I took a tiny bong load and started scarfing down a mountain of shrimp chow mein.

Sober, Esa spoke to me between mouthfuls of sweet and sour chicken.

"Any hot guys in your classes?"

"Just one...I wouldn't call him hot though. He's more...handsome."

"What's the difference?"

"Hotness fades. Handsomeness and beauty don't."

"Who is he? Where'd you meet him?"

"His name's Ben. He's tall, pale, and takes painting class with me."

"I think I know the guy. He sits next to me in Poli-Sci."

"No shit?" Now I got excited.

"Nah, I'm just kidding." Esa laughed and so did Molly, overhearing our conversation from the bathroom.

"*Stupid...*" I sneered.

The news on TV was covering a non-aggression treaty between Russia and Ukraine. For the longest time, there seemed to be no end to the conflict between the two countries as Russia was trying to muscle into their neighbor's resources. Everyone knew there was enough oil under that Ukrainian soil to make whoever got to it first the richest nation in the world.

"Aww, see that, girls? World peace is on its way." Esa beamed.

"Yeah, right," I snarled.

"You don't think so? If Russia and Ukraine can settle their problems, why's it so far-fetched?"

"This is merely a strategic move by Russia in a larger chess game. Furthermore, so long as the Middle East is politically and economically malleable, the American military-industrial complex will use war to mold it. I won't even get into North Korea and China."

"But."

"*Terrorism.*"

"But."

"*American-armed Inter-Middle Eastern genocide.*"

"Okay, I get it. Stop."

I started laughing but Esa didn't think it was so funny...she looked frightened. That stupid little hippie, I don't know how her courses haven't made her more pessimistic by now. Esa finished her food and got up off the couch, taking her dishes to the kitchen sink.

"I'm going to bed."

"Aw, come on, I was only messing around."

Esa didn't respond, dashing back to her room as quickly as possible. I heard Molly flush the toilet and wash her hands before opening the door to step out into the living room. She leaned against the doorframe and tilted her head to glare at me.

"Why'd you have to scare her like that?"

"I wasn't trying to...*I SAID SORRY.*"

"You're a very smart girl, Charlotte. Maybe too smart for your own good."

"Whatever, I won't talk at all then. No one needs to hear what I think."

Molly rolled her eyes, shook her head, and completed the trifecta with a sigh. She headed back to her room, leaving me with the Chinese food and TV for the night. I kept watching the news to soak in every last bit of this peace before it was long forgotten.

Chapter Seven

Man

I liked Charlotte from the moment we met. I took that moment and spun all sorts of imagined layers around it until it became a different memory altogether. Writers are obsessive, whether it be about love or words. My daydreams of her were all based in romance and not sex. In kisses, in holding hands, in eye contact, in living and dying for her. I preemptively bought all sorts of gifts online that I could give her, books on puppetry, paintbrushes, DVDs. It was only until that night, when I found myself two hundred dollars poorer, that I thought going on a shopping spree for a girl I just met made me a weirdo, or at least a fool. When feelings develop this quickly, the connection never meets the expectation.

~ * ~

I handed in my two-person play to my playwriting teacher that Wednesday. I wrote it in under ten minutes and printed it in red ink as a nod to his Marxist leanings. Like I said before, it took place in a dungeon, between two men talking about their wives who lived on the outside. At the end of the play, we learn both wives were imaginary but gave their husbands their only hope to live.

Russian literature class began with Tolstoy's heady drama and felt like slugging through knee-deep gulag snow goulash. Poetry class consisted of a thoughtless lecture on Walt Whitman. I could feel the sea breeze and the musty history in the words but nothing moved me.

I had been waiting for my class with Charlotte all day. At one point,

I walked by men painting the side of a building white and the smell nearly gave me a hard-on. Stepping into the studio a few seconds late, I saw that she was sitting on the same stool as the day before. Next to her, the stool I had sat in was taken by another guy, shorter but more muscular and confidant than me. Charlotte waved at me and mouthed "*Hey*," and I waved back and nodded, taking another seat at the opposite end of the room.

Our lecture was an introduction to blending with oil paint. Afterward, we began painting a still life of the same wine bottle, peach, and flower arrangement. With my skills a bit rusty, I unintentionally veered my painting out of the representational, into the abstract.

"Is that a lemon?" Charlotte asked about the peach, startling me a bit when I turned and realized she was right behind me.

"*Pfft. No.* Is that really what it looks like?"

"Like a rotting lemon."

I shrugged, accepting my creation's death, then kept decaying the fruit with browns.

"Don't get discouraged, I'm not doing much better on my end."

I turned around to look at her painting and saw the most perfectly painted photograph on canvas.

"Are you kidding? That's yours?"

"Yeah, what about it?"

"It's amazing. You didn't say anything about being *that* talented."

"I'm kinda good at everything. Sculpting, drawing…"

"Glass blowing?"

"I wish… *Do you smoke?*"

"All right class, back to your seats…these paintings aren't going to finish themselves," the instructor shouted, looking at Charlotte.

"We'll talk later," Charlotte said as she strolled back to her stool.

Once class was finished, I packed my things and waited for her. When she was ready to go, she floated over to continue exactly where we left off.

"Do you want to smoke with me right now?"

"Sure."

We went outside and I pulled out a pack of Camels. I opened it up to take out two, one for me and the lucky for her.

"Oh, I didn't mean cigarettes."

I lit mine up regardless.

"You smoke crack?"

Charlotte snorted through a laugh.

"*No*, jackass, *weed*."

"Oh. I don't like getting stoned."

"Really? Why not? It's great."

"I start acting very foolish."

"So what? Everybody does."

"I really don't enjoy it."

"Leave it to me, I'll pack you a bowl that will change your mind about weed."

"I'll come with you…but I won't smoke."

"We'll see about that."

We found an empty parking lot and Charlotte took out a pipe she kept in her secret pocket. She loaded it up with weed that looked like it was covered in sea salt and vermillion silk.

She took the hit, passed it my way and I pushed it back. She shrugged and we each stuck to smoking our respective plants. The breeze carried the smoke so whimsically we just watched it in a silence that wasn't one bit awkward. We said our goodbyes and though they felt platonic, I left more attracted to her than I could have been to anyone.

Chapter Eight

Woman

I was a bit cottonmouthed and had to grab a sip of water from the drinking fountain before heading into class. As I turned a corner and approached the fountain, I saw Ben bent over the buzzing dispenser, slurping. He stood up straight then turned to me, wiping his lips dry.

"How are you, Charlotte?"

I don't know what it was but suddenly, I had a rush of pleasure shoot up my body. I nearly swooned.

"Good," I gulped.

"Did you save a seat for me this time?"

"Not yet."

"So, you will then? Thanks."

Ben strolled away as if someone was calling him. I stood there paralyzed, watching him move along until I almost forgot I was thirsty. After a few big gulps, I rushed into the classroom to reserve two seats. I found two empty stools and took one. The same guy that sat next to me last class tried to pull a fast one and sat in Ben's stool again. I had to put the idiot in check.

"Beat it, pal. Seat's taken."

"Seriously?"

"You think I'm kidding?"

"Wow, you're so fucking rude."

"Cool, now find a different stool, creep."

"Bitch."

He walked away flustered enough to spend the rest of the day analyzing himself. Ben entered the classroom and came right to me, sitting down in the stool I fought for his ass to perch on.

"Thanks, Charlotte."

"You're welcome."

Painting doesn't require much thought so I didn't have trouble completing the assignment and letting Ben consume my mind. I wondered when he was going to make a move, if he was thinking of me, if he would figure out clever ways to touch me. He would try to steal glances at me when I wasn't looking and I pretended not to catch him every time.

"What's your favorite movie?" I asked him.

"Anything by Fellini. Especially *Satyricon*."

"Who's that?"

"An old Italian filmmaker."

"Oh, is he artsy?"

"Yeah, that's the kind of stuff I like."

"I like David Lynch. He makes films like that."

"He sure does."

"Tim Burton."

"He's great too."

"What about music? Who do you listen to?"

"Pretty much everything but mostly jazz."

"Really. I don't hear that answer too often."

"That's a shame. Do you listen to jazz?"

"No. Just punk rock."

"Jazz players were punk rock before anyone came up with a title."

"How so?"

"They lived crazy, genius, genuine lives. People don't know how to live that way anymore, with such over-the-top, spontaneous comedy and tragedy."

"Not even you?"

He looked at me with a smirk.

"I'm an exception."

"I am too."

We chit-chatted through class until exiting the studio side by side when he turned to me with anxiety flooding out of every pore. I was flattered he was so unnerved by the idea of asking out little old me.

"Say Charlotte, if you're interested, maybe sometime you'd like to go to a movie or a jazz show, I think that would be pretty cool."

"Sure, Ben. Maybe we could *both* go."

"Umm…yeah…like the two of us…I meant that. That would be amazing." He shone with virginal enthusiasm.

"Just let me know when."

"Okay."

He stood there stupefied so I helped him out an inch.

"Do you want my number?"

"Oh yeah, of course…"

He pulled out his flip-phone and that's when I knew he was the one for me.

"Wow, *old school.*"

"Yeah, I don't buy into the whole 'smart' epidemic."

"Good for you. You're stronger than me."

"I doubt it but thanks."

I swallowed hard and told him my number. "718-401-2141."

"I'll text you so that you can have mine."

"Cool."

"See you soon."

"Yeah. Soon."

I wished he waited to walk me home before asking me out and forcing us to split. Oh well, I guess for now, this future I see us living will keep my mind occupied. It's a future that is becoming clearer every day.

Chapter Nine

Man

It seemed as though my father had a sixth sense of the whereabouts of his son because the moment I stepped back into my dorm, I received a call from him.

"Hey Pop," I answered.

Before saying anything, he gasped, struggling to breathe.

"Benjamin, there's been a tragedy," choking up, his voice sounded tearful.

The bottom fell from under me. My heart sunk into my stomach. I felt somehow more human in this moment, awaiting the death blow.

"What happened?" I asked.

He started sobbing over the phone. Blubbering through his words and forcing me to cry with him out of pure confusion.

"It's your mother."

"Is she all right?"

"No, Ben. She's not all right. She died, son. Your mother is gone."

I fell backward onto my couch, hysterically crying and thrashing about. I put the phone down but he could still hear my shrieking.

"Benjamin." I heard him calling for me and picked the phone back up to my ear.

"What?"

"You need to come home as soon as possible. Your brother will pay for your flight."

I needed a second to recalibrate my mind.

"I'll pack light and find a flight for tonight."

"I'll be waiting for you."

"How did she…"

"Heart attack. At fifty-six…she was so young. Had so much life in her. I don't understand."

I was shaking terribly, snot and tears streaming down my face. I wished the pain could be replaced with a bleeding wound. I had the task of arranging my passage home but I was barely stable enough to dial my brother's number. The phone rang three times before he finally answered.

"Are you all right, Ben?"

"Yes," I whimpered, half-unhinged.

"She didn't suffer, Ben."

"What do you mean? She had a heart attack."

"In her sleep."

"She's been dead all day and Dad only told me now?"

"He didn't want to disturb you in school. We both thought it was best you came home first."

"Jerry, I need you to arrange my flight. I can't do it."

"You can't do what?"

"I can't get on a computer and find a fucking flight to take me to my mother's funeral."

"Are you sure you're all right, Ben? I don't need to call you help, do I?"

"You seem to be taking this rather well, Jerry."

"The hell I am. I've been crying all day."

"I need you to arrange my flight."

"Okay, okay. I'm going to text you the information as soon as I book it. Be ready to leave for the airport within the hour."

"I'm ready now."

"Good. I'll see you tomorrow."

"Bye."

My family always considered me the sensitive one. Funny, I rarely ever talked to them so I wasn't sure how they would know. They saw me as a translucent bottle, seeing through my neutral exterior into the sea of tears behind the glass. My sadness gave them no cause for alarm. They were sure I wouldn't be affected by the same traumas that drive other young men toward violence. That, I suppose, is one of the benefits to being poor. You see all these young, sheltered kids snapping after a shoelace breaks, meanwhile a poor kid lives through ten times the horror and never makes a peep.

My brother texted me ten minutes later. My flight was leaving in three hours. I was out the door in three minutes. I took nothing with me but my wallet, phone, and keys. I forgot my cigarettes but I figured strangers would be able to tell by my grief-ridden, blubbering face, I earned one to bum.

A German Ernte 23 cigarette outside the airport stroked my nerves steady. Feeling lonelier than a dying hermit, I watched the planes flee the earth, never sure they would return. There was a heavy fog that night, embracing me into one grey world. My emotional affliction gave me much trouble going through security. I absorbed any questions they pressed me with like broken glass into quicksand. Waiting in the terminal, I spoke to no one and hid in my jacket. Boarding the plane, I knew I'd have to keep it together for as long as I was in that airtight tubing. If I chose to let it all come bitching out of me, screaming about how my mother's role as housewife devolved into slavery. How we all resented my father's drinking and absence. How my wealthy brother left us high and dry. Then my unlucky fellow passengers might actually give my wallowing the time of day. I chose to spare them, figuring these people were already escaping from or returning to their own tragedies.

Landing, my brother met me outside the terminal. Already having waited fifteen minutes in his car, he seemed bothered, like I was guilty from the get-go.

"Hey." He nodded and peeled away from the pickup lane.

"Wish we could've seen each other under better circumstances."

"Guess this is how we learn...Mom always said we should be closer," he replied, with an uncanny ability to be snarky in any situation.

"She'd be happy we're together now."

"Yeah."

We drove in silence on the sober highways. Luxury cars like this one glide so pristinely it's like traveling in a ghost carriage.

"Do you believe in ghosts, Jerry?"

"No, Ben. Our mom is not a fucking ghost."

"I didn't say she was."

"There are no ghosts. There's no heaven or hell."

"Heaven and hell are states of mind."

"You think your mind can be heaven? You haven't lived long enough, Ben."

"Sure, it can, Jerry. *You* haven't lived long enough."

That was the last word and though there was no familial closeness between us, the glory of besting him with words felt almost as good.

We parked outside our dad's apartment complex and walked up the stairs to the lobby. Dialing my father up on the callbox, he simply buzzed us in and didn't bother greeting us over the phone. Our father opened the door crying, in nothing but his boxers. Too emotionally exhausted for pants, he grabbed us both and pressed us against his hairy body in a pained and tired hug.

"She loved you both so much. I know you two aren't friendly but promise me, for this time, we will be a family again. Life is too short to be fighting all the time. You both know how you truly feel about one another, inside you don't hate each other. I want you to say it now. Each of you, tell the other you love them."

"That's all right, Dad. Ben knows how I feel."

Jerry shot my father down without hesitation. The old man didn't back down though. He grabbed Jerry by the back of the neck with such firmness that each meaty old finger curled around a different disk in Jerry's vertebrae.

"I'm not letting you in my house until you tell Ben that you love him."

"What's wrong with you? We're brothers, after all… I love *you*, Jerry. Sheesh, that wasn't so hard." It was easier to say now that it made him look bad.

"Love you too, Ben." He winced.

"Your mother would've been so happy to hear that."

"She's here in spirit, Dad."

"Yeah, right. Your mother hated this apartment. If her spirit is anywhere, it's on fucking vacation. Now get your asses in here and make yourselves at home."

We went inside and were hit with a new stench. We had adapted to the smell of our own home but that familiar mixture of our family's collective reek was now gone. The absence of us children removed our additions to the recipe and left it solely the combination of my mother and father. Now with her gone, it would degenerate to a smell all my father's, something similar to that foulness I'd pick up when I'd use the bathroom moments after him.

~ * ~

Our family always kept to ourselves. My brother and I never had friends over. Neither did my parents. I suppose the reason for this was because we were embarrassed of how we lived, poorly and without order.

This lack of order was the source of our poverty. Our family tenanted in chaos. That's why it was no surprise my mother's funeral, which was bankrolled by my brother, was attended only by us. Each empty pew in that temple was another steppe added to the mountain of shame looming over us. We never spoke of it but the shame was as a part of us as our skin.

After a solemn sermon, we buried her, each of us with a shovel, throwing dirt upon the past which we entombed in a plain wooden casket adorned with nothing. We didn't stop until there was a layer of dirt covering her completely. I was burying part of myself with her, the part of myself that was inauthentic. My culture, upbringing, every prejudice I had in favor or against anything, gone. As if sensing this upheaval within me, my father put his hand on my shoulder and passed down a new commandment.

"This is going to change you for the rest of your life but one thing it can't change is that you're a Jew. You were born a Jew and you will die a Jew. I swear upon your mother's fresh grave, it is her only wish and mine, you marry a Jew someday."

Love couldn't just satisfy me anymore. It now had to satisfy those that came before me.

Chapter Ten

Woman

I hadn't gotten a call or text from Ben since he asked me out. Wednesday finally rolled around and I returned to that same stool. I saw him walk into painting class, glance at me, avert his eyes, then take a seat at a different end of the studio. It was the most heartbreaking feeling I've ever known up to that point. The quiet death of potential. Everything I've been taught made me feel like I wasn't entitled to cry over a guy I barely knew. Still, I couldn't paint, I couldn't sit, and I couldn't talk to anyone. I just took my bag and bailed. For someone who claims to be clairvoyant, I don't know how I didn't see this coming. The thought that the man who was supposed to be my husband abandoned his destiny was worse than dying. Swiftly leaving campus, I would look over my shoulder every few seconds, hoping to see him running after me, calling my name, but he was nowhere.

I returned to my dorm and fell into my pillow to soak it in tears. After about an hour, I turned to the only remedy I knew, puppets. I started shaving away at a new piece of wood, all night carving new features of a skull. Whose skull? Mine, but not the Charlotte you know. No, this was the Charlotte Ben reduced me to. The me I would be without him. The puppet was skinny and shriveled and covered in wrinkle rivets and even though it was only wooden, you could tell it was dying in some organic way. I missed all my Thursday classes to stay in bed, my blanket was covered in shavings as I completed the doll. When I finally left my room the next day, Molly and Esa were waiting for me.

"What's wrong, babe? You've been cooped up in there for two

days," Esa asked.

"He doesn't want me anymore." I stooped into both of their embraces and started crying again.

"Bastard," Esa sneered.

"How do you know? Did he say that?" Molly asked.

"No."

"How can you be sure?" Molly continued.

"He wouldn't sit next to me or even say hi. He looked at me and turned away like I was some fucking stranger."

"That might not mean he doesn't want you."

"What else could it mean?"

"That he doesn't want to talk to anyone."

I pulled out of their arms and looked into Molly's eyes. "Why wouldn't he?" I asked, perplexed.

"Maybe he's hurt. Maybe he's sick. Only he knows. Is he the type of guy that would keep his feelings inside?"

"Ben Weiss suppresses so much, he could explode at any moment."

"Weiss? He's Jewish?" Esa asked.

"Yeah."

"You never said anything about him being a Jew. That changes everything."

"What are you talking about? What does it change?"

"Dude…everything," Molly chimed in.

"That's right, Charlotte. Jews stay inside the clan. They might fuck other kinds of girls but they only marry other Jews."

"How do you know? Did you ever date one?"

"Honestly, I never saw one up close until college, but I knew other girls who tried what you're doing and they all ended up with broken hearts."

"You haven't even started dating him yet, so imagine how bad it's gonna hurt when he dumps you later in the relationship," Esa added.

"You can't paint the whole religion with the same brush. What about all the half Jews in the world?"

"There are exceptions to every rule but the exception is never worth chasing."

"Look, I'm not going to drop this guy based on how you think all Jews act."

"Jews like bossy women. Maybe if you were bossier, he'd like you again," Molly suggested.

"Really?"

"It's worth a shot. What do you have to lose?"

"I guess."

"See, Charlotte, Esa and I may not be experts in Jews but we're experts in you and we know that you'll cave and end up taking our advice almost every time."

They laughed like I wasn't even in the room, high-fiving each other. This should've offended me but something about the joy they received at my expense made me smile.

"What do you think my chances are of actually hooking up with this guy?"

"Thirty percent," said Esa.

"Ten percent...which is better than plenty of other bitches would get," Molly continued.

~ * ~

I went to class determined to speak to Ben. There was no way he could avoid me once we got to talking. I saw him smoking outside the classroom and again he averted his eyes. I stormed up to him with casual speed.

"How come you didn't say hi to me last class? Are you avoiding me?"

His lip flinched as he exhaled smoke. I wasn't sure if this was a nervous tick or if he actually said something so quietly that no human could possibly hear it.

"Maybe," he said, "I suppose so," he reiterated.

"Why would you be avoiding me?"

"I don't know."

The conversation halted to a standstill. He knew how to exhaust any argument, thus winning.

"Sit next to me today. We should talk."

He quietly shrugged then put out his cigarette to follow me into the classroom. Perhaps Molly and Esa were right. He was already responding to female domination. We sat in our usual spots and I thought of what move to make next and figured I might as well go right for the jugular.

"You can be honest with me, you know. We haven't been friends long but I think I can help you."

He stared at me with a blankness the average person might not give any significance to but to me, it indicated a deep ache in him, as if his pain had ironed out any wrinkle of emotion from him.

"What makes you think I'm not being honest?"

"You're a smart guy, Ben. You write, you read, you watch foreign films, listen to jazz. Why are your answers so simple? Is what you really think and feel so complex that you don't even know how to talk about it?"

He swallowed hard.

"Well, whenever you're ready you can talk to me."

"Okay," he coughed out.

"Good. Just remember, Ben, I can't read your mind."

The lesson of the day was about landscape painting. I chose to paint an autumn scene and Ben chose to paint a forest lake. Both paintings turned out swell and after class we carried them proudly as we walked together.

"So, about that movie," I started.

"I need to be alone right now."

"Why?"

"Because last week I lost my mother," he said it casually, with no care for what kind of unwanted attention I'd pay him.

I turned to him, staring squarely at his face and in his eyes, taking in all of him while simultaneously sinking into my own pit.

"I'm sorry…That's so terrible. If there's anything…"

"Yeah, can you take my painting with you?"

"With me where?"

"Back wherever you go."

"You really don't want it?"

"I want you to have it."

He handed me his landscape and now, like a jackass, I was carrying two canvases, making sure my hands wouldn't touch the wet paint on either.

"I have to be alone now. There's nothing left to say."

"Call me if you need anything."

"Okay."

He sped away so fast I couldn't catch up to him unless I ran. I was back on the path home, alone again, encumbered with two paintings, both consuming me with thoughts of Ben that lasted me into the night. I hung them up on my wall side by side and imagined they were us, holding hands. I lay in bed and shed a few tears. I knew if I ever lost my mother, I'd be an emotional wreck for months afterward. If I even survived. As much as I wanted to comfort him, what I needed at this moment was comforting myself. I needed someone to remind me that life has meaning in a world where such a terrible thing could happen to such a kind and gentle boy as Ben Weiss.

Chapter Eleven

Man

Alone in my dorm, time moving at a stepped-on snail's pace, for months I kept to myself, speaking to no one. I committed my life to writing and viewed my youth as the necessary sacrifice to the gods in exchange for talent and success. Had I not made this sacrifice, I'd probably end up yet another old man rotted by work. I had no desires to go out drinking, make lifelong friends, or have a girlfriend.

I'd write novels, screenplays, short stories, and poetry. I'd paint the most insane and surrealistic depictions of hell. The dining dead, picking upon a Thanksgiving swine, inside the open belly of some living abomination. Wretches and demons blessed with the heads of birds upon their tortured bodies. Butter knives spreading melted mothers upon the ashen black bread human toast. A man with a mandolin for an ass, blood-soaked strings played by blood thirsty tyrants. These images swirling in my head, I knew what I once told my brother was correct: hell is a state of mind.

If I spat on my mother's grave by falling in love with Charlotte, would I be sentenced to hell? Would I be committing some egregious sin? Breaking a commandment? Honor thy mother and father. Then again, all Jews go to hell according to the dominant religions of this world, anyway. This reality we exist in might be a deceptive layer of illusion fabricated by Satan. So, why not give my children a fighting chance at salvation through Christ and marry the girl? Why not give up the struggle for some imagined ideal of what my family should look like and what my love should be? If her God isn't mine, is her reality mine? Regardless of my dilemma, thinking of her was the most mind-altering intoxicant, my mind's perfume when on Charlotte.

My pile of books dwindled down to a mere fifty pages. I could pinch those fifty pages and feel my thumbnail pressing against my index finger. The more books I finished, the more truth I hoarded. People who don't read are blind to the signs that foretell the future. They protest our heroes then praise our villains. Myths play out in the world every day but people don't have the toolset to recognize them.

They say it takes your body about seven years to replace every cell but I felt like reading these books had expedited the process and made it take seven weeks. I decided to become a being that was totally myself. The first step was removing everyone from my life. I deleted all my social media accounts and texted the most brutal relationship-ending truths to all my old friends. I even cut off my own family. Soon no one but Charlotte was left for me to sever ties with. I saved her for last because I knew she'd be the most difficult to remove, like pulling teeth. I decided I would call her out of the blue.

"Ben?"

"Hey, Charlotte."

"You never call me, what's up?"

"I needed to talk to you."

"Go for it."

"I was in love with you."

"*Was?*"

"Yes. I couldn't stop thinking about you. I wanted to pull my heart out of my chest just to make the feeling stop. It was so intense."

"I know, Ben."

"You know?"

"Girls aren't stupid, Ben. We know when guys like us. Sheesh, don't you have any self-awareness?"

"I have more self-awareness than anyone you know."

She laughed out loud so hard it felt like the phone's connection was breaking.

"Is that all you called to tell me?" She asked.

"No."

"What else?"

"I wanted to tell you that I won't be speaking to you anymore. So, don't bother trying to start up conversation."

"Is this a prank?"

"No."

"Just because your mom died doesn't mean you have to become a jerk. I don't have a dad but you don't see me treating people like shit."

"I don't know you well enough...maybe you do."

Her pause awarded me victory.

"You're not even upset that I brought up your mom? You're numb."

"Save the analysis for someone that gives a shit."

"I'll see you tomorrow," she said, refusing to accept my cruelty.

I hung up the phone smiling. Not because I was finally free of her. Quite the opposite. I was smiling because I thought she was adorable. With a heavy sigh, I tried to return to my work but I was more exhausted to create great literature as great literature was exhausted to be created. I could feel every finger slightly less potent with my usual genius. She ruined my plans for the evening. Classics would go unwritten. Masterpieces never manifested. How many great works, theories, and salvations were lost just because some poor, brilliant sap fell madly in love with a girl.

Chapter Twelve

Woman

I spent the whole night after that phone call crying but by morning, I promised myself I would tell Ben I loved him. If he were to reject me again then I would never shed another tear for him. I met him outside class where he was sulking in the shadows, staring down at the ground.

"You're either going to talk to me or you're just going to have to drop out of this class."

"You've got some nerve."

"You're mistaken. It's called balls. I can understand why you can't tell the difference."

"What do you want from me?"

"The world is coming to an end in our lifetimes. I know this because I can see the future. Call me crazy all you like but it is the truth. Now, we can either spend that time stupidly trying to figure our lives out, going nowhere because we made the wrong choices or we can be happy spending the rest of our brief lives together starting today."

"Wow…and I thought I was crazy."

"I love you, Ben Weiss. I am madly in love with you and I know you are still in love with me."

At that moment, his lower eyelid and bottom lip twitched in sync as if I pushed him toward some kind of breakthrough. My hope was that hearing those three little words would release him from his prison.

"I'm Jewish, Charlotte. I can't be with you," he blurted out.

He resorted to this excuse just to rid himself of the discomfort of dealing with his emotions.

What was I supposed to say now? I didn't want to disrespect his religion and call him a pussy. This was exactly what Molly and Esa warned me about. They were right, it's better it happened now than later. Through some incredible mastery of will, I forced myself not to give a shit. I pretended it was one big relief. That now we could both stop pretending and resume our lives.

"That's fine, Ben. If you don't have it in you, your loss. Good luck with everything."

I turned around and walked into class.

"Don't have *what* in me?"

I didn't answer. Just like him, I would employ the tactic of inaction to my benefit. He was out of my life and pushed to my periphery. When I got home, I tore Ben's painting off my wall and repeatedly stabbed it with a sharp knife, then tossed the canvas out the window. At that moment, my expectations, desires, and dreams changed. I accepted that my clairvoyance did not determine my destiny and that no matter what I saw in a vision, I could take actions to alter that future. I'm sure the next time I see the man of my dreams, he will not be an artist, he will be athletic and fit. He will be smart but simple. He won't be so full of himself and most importantly, he'll be willing to talk to me.

Part Two

Chapter Thirteen

Man

Six years since graduating college with a Bachelor's in English, I became exactly what I wanted to be, a struggling writer in a cranberry beanie living in a madness-inducing-sized studio apartment. I get strange looks and sneers from strangers on the street as my skeleton walks inside me and the rest of my flesh goes along for the ride. I could have been born for a slew of other careers and lived much more fabulously. I could've been a lawyer, doctor, or been handed down a cushy gig in real estate. Whatever though, so long as I can afford a drink and a pack of cigarettes every day, I have nothing to complain about. I never wanted to be a journalist but it seems it's the only kind of writing that brings in money or readers. People only respond to headlines. One has to be a slinger of slug lines to make an impact.

Still, I keep thinking it's only a matter of time until everything changes and I write the book that I'll be remembered for. It'll fly off the shelves and the people will catch my drift like a virus. Even though I don't consider myself a great writer. I'm actually rather useless. There are junkies shooting up all day contributing more to society than I do. I don't even know how to suffer properly. I'm not an artist, I'm a hack. I'll probably end up one of those tortured geniuses so poor he's eating dog food out the can until hundreds of years after I'm gone when I'll be rediscovered as a philosopher whose ideas inspire new schools of thought.

I remember my mother's parting wish that I marry a Jewish woman.

Even though the majority of them, based on their similar upbringings as sheltered princesses, make me cringe. I met one just the other night, smoking a cigarette outside of a synagogue as the service was ending and waiting for all the well-dressed tail to come uniformly spilling out. I dressed so they would think I wasted my night in temple with them. When they'd see my height and gentile style, they'd find me quite exciting. The first I spoke to, Natasha, was a cute Russian Jew. She was slender and tall and with absolutely nothing unique about her personality whatsoever. She didn't have talent or interests other than watching television and shopping in West Hollywood. We made plans for dinner on a night I completed an article about the rise of BDSM in the era of big government. With the topic fresh on my mind, I was afraid I'd have nothing tasteful to discuss over pasta. It was just my luck she decided to be the one to ask all the questions.

"So, what do you do for work?"

It's been my experience this is the foremost qualifier into a woman's heart. Your income, car, and credit. The holy trinity of materialism. Philosophy and art are second, if not absolutely irrelevant to them.

"I'm a journalist and struggling novelist."

"What does that mean? Struggling?"

"It means I've written books but haven't sold them."

She looked at me blankly, wondering where all the men with normal jobs in Los Angeles went.

"Do you have any roommates?" she continued, moving on.

"No, I live in a small studio apartment all by myself."

"Oh…that must suck."

"Actually, I love it. Where do you live?"

"With my parents."

I nodded plainly.

"Do you have any favorite books?"

"I don't read. I mean, I can but I don't."

"Do you watch TV?"

"How'd you know?"

"Good guess."

"What's my favorite show?" she asked.

"*The Big Bang Theory?*"

"*Oh my God*...did you stalk me on Facebook?"

"No. I guessed the dumbest show I could think of."

I made myself laugh so hard I snorted. She blushed with embarrassment, realizing a half second too late how stupid she was.

"Just kidding." I had to soften the blow before she simply left the dinner table. "I love that show too."

"Have you ever been to Israel?" she asked.

Here we go, I thought.

"Nope," I answered.

"You know you can go for free, right? I did over the summer. It was life changing."

"I wouldn't go if they paid me."

"You're not one of those self-hating Jews, are you?"

"I hate myself but it has nothing to do with being Jewish. I had a friend who went to Israel and he told me it all feels like a crusades-themed Disneyland. You get the sense someone is making money off intentionally forcing these people who hate each other to live together. He said without the hatred, the tourism would suffer."

She didn't know what to make of me or my beliefs. She just knew she would never see me again and I knew that too. I couldn't wait. After she got in her Uber, I lifted my head up to the sky, staring through the smog as if asking my mother how much longer I had to suffer trying to appease her. I heard a voice inside my head that sounded like hers and it told me that all these girls needed to fuck off, and if I found someone who was actually interesting it didn't matter what religion she was. So be it, if my mother changed her mind, wanting me to be with a gentile, I had no choice but to honor her wishes. To gentile girls I would seem exotic. They would not take my Jewishness for granted.

No matter what your origin, race, religion, or ethnicity, you should never feel obligated to procreate with your kind. We're not here to breed children like dogs. It's better to mix and make new combinations the world has never seen before. Black girls fuck Asian guys. Asian women fuck Black men. White ladies fuck black gentlemen. Black chicks fuck white dudes. White fools fuck Latina broads. Latin homies fuck white babes.

Jews bang Muslims. Have as little prejudice for your lover's background as the homosexuals do. The only way you can be yourself is to reject everything you didn't teach you.

~ * ~

A guy I went to high school with, Jimmy Keenan, saw me inside the liquor mart across the street from my apartment. I was second in line, waiting to buy a pack of smokes when Jimmy saw me.

"Oh shit, Ben? Ben Weiss?"

"Jimmy?" I answered, less enthused.

"Fuck yeah, you remember."

"Tone it down with the cursing, I come here every day."

"My bad, everybody, sorry," he panned his apologizing shrug around the mart. He never grew out of his sad-clown antics.

"Thanks."

I got to the front of the line and bought my cigarettes. Jimmy stayed put as if trying to cut behind me.

"You can't cut the line behind me, Jimmy. These people have been waiting."

"That's not what I'm doing, man. I wanted to buy some smokes too, same ones as you actually. Do you mind if I bum a couple instead of buying my own?"

"Yes. I mind."

"Just three cigarettes, I'll give you a dollar."

"Fine."

I pulled three cigarettes out of the box and handed them to him. He passed me a freshly-minted dollar bill and I stuffed it into my back pocket, aging it immediately, reducing its value.

"Thank you, fuck you, bye." I nodded at Jimmy, smiling so wide he couldn't take offense.

"Wait. Let's smoke one together. Right now. Outside," Jimmy begged me.

"I got places to be, Jim."

"I wanna hear all about it."

He followed me out, right on my heels and as I lit up, so did he. The stoplight turned red, giving me no choice but to tolerate him.

"Everybody still talks about you, Ben. We all heard about your mom but you kinda disappeared, so no one was able to reach out to you."

"Yeah well, that's how I like it."

"What do you do now?"

"Nothing mostly. I smoke."

"Always the jokester. Let me guess. You do standup."

"No."

"Me, I do insurance. You ever need any life, car, earthquake, or home insurance just give me a ring. Times are too fucked up not to think ahead. Here's my card."

The light changed and we both crossed to the other side of the street. Halfway through, he shoved his card in my face but with one angry look, he knew to stuff it right back where the sun doesn't shine.

"Or, just tell me your number. I'll remember it."

"No thanks, I'll find you if I need you," I replied.

We stopped in front of my apartment complex and I walked to the door with my keys already out. I couldn't leave his side fast enough.

"We should get dinner sometime, Ben. I know this really good Indian place around here, appetizers, entrées, dessert, all on me."

"Sorry, Jimmy."

I opened the door and swiftly left him but he kept staring at me through the glass lobby door as I took the elevator out of his life. I didn't belong at any sit-down dinner with anyone I went to high school with. I didn't belong in that high school at all. I was the charity case that only afforded tuition because my dad took three jobs. I was on financial aid and had a scholarship. Still we struggled paying for everything. I was the only person in my entire graduating class to pursue the arts seriously. Everybody else realized more quickly than I did that having something to say won't get you rich. Some kids came close, like directors that went into commercials and fine artists that took to fashion. But me, I was the only one trying to make undiluted musings about the nature of this existence. Looking back on it now, Dad spent all that time working for nothing.

I soon learned Jimmy asked around and found out which apartment

I lived in. He would send me letters in the mail as if we were having small talk in person. Every letter was stained and stinky. These letters would fill me in on who married who, who had kids, who's rich, who's poor. Lives to compare to mine. One girl in particular, Selma Bloom, was the girl everyone had a crush on. After high school she became a model, dating around Los Angeles until finally landing an older, fat celebrity. *What a waste,* I thought. She gave up trying to find love and settled on security. Although he didn't have a wife or a good job, Jimmy's claim to fame was all the places he'd traveled, almost all of Western Europe, Russia, China, Japan, Thailand, South Korea, India, Brazil, Chile, Argentina, Mexico, Canada, all fifty American states. Having never made enough money to finance such expeditions, my own travels consisted of regular trips to Las Vegas and San Francisco, two places I consider siblings to Los Angeles. San Francisco being the older sister and Las Vegas being the younger brother. If you think about it, Los Angeles shows all the signs of middle-sibling syndrome. I had incredible luck meeting girls in either city. I would hang out at dark bars, stick out like a sore thumb minding my own business, and the hungry ones would always hover over. Once they heard my laugh, they wanted to be around me, buying me drinks. Jimmy's letters made me feel sorry for myself. I was long overdue for a lay. So, I decided I was taking a trip. I wrote Jimmy back for the first time, saying, *Do not write me this week. I'll be away.*

I took a Greyhound to San Francisco. Twenty bucks for a one-way trip. Just in case I met someone worth never coming home for. The first place I stopped was a bar right by the armory, a historic building the deviants converted into a sex palace. I didn't want to go inside but I did want to absorb its forbidden energy by drinking at the bar next door. I ordered my usual. Cold red wine. I didn't specify a grape. It was all the same to me. I would've drunk it straight from the bottle if they had let me but this was San Francisco. When it tries to be classy it's twice as elegant as Los Angeles. When it tries to be 'real,' San Francisco is three times as wretched, desperate, and nihilistic. Watching me from the other side of the bar was a woman with red hair and a single tattoo of a fountain pen over her left eye. She was nursing a martini in one hand and in the other she shuffled half a pack of cards, only the black ones. Noticing me staring out the window at the BDSM armory, she needed to ask me what my deal was.

"Are you a member?"

"I didn't know it was a club."

"You have to be good-looking to get invited."

"Where's the kink in that?"

"Some ugly people get accepted too, if they're talented."

"Didn't know ugly was a talent."

"Talented in domination, subordination, or just tolerance to pain."

"Emotional pain?"

"No."

"I suppose I wouldn't stand a crack rock's chance in San Francisco."

"You're very funny," she smiled.

"But you didn't laugh," I smiled back.

She sat down next me at that point.

"Drinking a red wine and staring out at the armory? Are you sure you're not a perv?"

"My perversion is I always tell the truth."

"What difference does your truth make if you're always wrong? Who was the last person you fucked?"

"A Jewish girl in Los Angeles. We were together a month before I got rid of her."

"Why'd you do that?"

"She would get so furious about the most menial shit that loving her became impossible."

"When was this?"

"Two years ago."

"You haven't fucked anyone in two years?"

"Besides myself, no."

"That explains why you're so curious."

"Does it? I suppose I do masturbate a lot. Sometimes four times a day but only to the tasteful stuff. The worst I catch myself watching is interracial lesbian."

"If that's bad then I'm filthy."

"Not true. You're just a typical San Franciscan."

"Would you consider yourself an expert at jerking off?"

"Just as much as any guy. Then again, things are starting to take longer so perhaps I've lost my touch."

"Always making jokes. Joking and jerking all the time. It's because you're so hurt all you can do is make other people laugh. Otherwise you're uncomfortable everywhere."

"You got me all figured out."

"*Oh no, no, no.* There's plenty of mystery to you left. It's one thing to know you are this way. It's another thing to see it. I'd bet getting you to open up emotionally is like watching a corpse plant bloom."

"How about we get out of here and I show you?"

"Let's go to my place. I don't live too far from here."

We strolled out the bar and I kept her entertained by my funny guy facade until we reached the foot of her bed where she let me sit. She stripped slowly, like how you'd expect a magician would. My eyes grew watery at the sight of her naked body.

"Kiss me," I demanded in an asking sort of way.

"No."

"Then what do we do?"

"You masturbate and I watch."

Off went my pants and shirt. Naked, I sprawled out on her bed, working my hand up and down my shaft. My anxiety kept me limp but when she began sticking a glass dildo into herself, it evaporated out of me. The thought of replacing that dildo with my cock, that my cock would satisfy her more than solid glass, made me stiffen to the hardness of stone. As it quivered there in my hand, standing straight, she moaned harder and harder watching every little throbbing beat. I came in a gush of white surrender and it was at this moment she was ready. She laid her bottle-shaped body beside mine, first gently combing her fingers through my pubic hair.

"You shot out quite a lot."

"This place always brings back a lot of memories."

"You think emotional reactions to places can make you cum harder?"

Before she could even hear my answer, her mouth was around my cock. Perhaps she was asking my balls and not me. Through sleight of hand, she magically made a condom appear and roll over my head, down my shaft, without her ever touching me. To no one's surprise, there was nothing magical about how I fucked her. After a while, it was evident I wasn't going to cum again.

"What's wrong? You can't go twice?"

"Honestly, I can't go once. I usually only cum when I masturbate."

"Don't worry, a lot of guys have that problem."

"Yeah, I don't feel like any less of a man or anything. It's 2020. People are sick. In fact, I feel like it makes me more of a writer."

"I doubt Hemingway had trouble cumming."

"Maybe not him but the weirdos I admire, I'd bet on it."

"I can see why you think that. You're so in your head that you're completely disconnected from your body. Something like that?"

"That works."

She laid beside me, tightly holding my limp body all night. Around four-thirteen a.m., I realized tears were running down my cheeks but I couldn't exactly say why. Laying there, sensing the presence of all the people I ever touched, my mind was consumed with all the turbulence that brought me to this bed. She stirred awake, looked at me and even in the dark, could tell something was wrong.

"Don't cry, you're the most beautiful person I've ever met."

The comment didn't sit right with me but the moment called for silence. She wiped away the tears she sensed were on my cheek and fell back to sleep. Meanwhile, my torment saw no end. I was in some kind of droning state of waking nightmare, mind bleeding till the San Francisco sun rose. I stayed with her another day and night, having sex three more times and not cumming once. She came six times though, each from oral. Once it was time for me to go, she wanted to arrange some kind of long-distance relationship but I couldn't commit to it. She only wanted to love me so she could understand what was wrong with me.

I returned to Los Angeles and the first thing I did when I arrived at my apartment building was check my mail for anything from Jimmy. The box was empty and, in that moment, for the first time, I finally realized I couldn't go on so alone.

Chapter Fourteen

Woman

Los Angeles is no New York. This city closes too early and people don't have enough wisdom to properly use the time while it's open. Alas, this is where television is filmed and I work in television, doing exactly what I said I was going to do, playing with puppets. If you've ever seen *Hamburger Hotdog*, I play the Goose. It's not my voice but it's my hand inside that body. Jinx isn't handling the move well either. He hates the heat, hates my apartment, and most of all, hates how I don't let him stay out all night like he used to in Brooklyn. I haven't even mentioned the worst thing, which is that everyone drives because the public transportation system is shit and everything is so spread out. Every morning to get to work, I have to either order a ride or get one from a coworker.

Guys in Los Angeles date in real life like they're interacting with you on a dating app. They'll sit right across from a girl, look into her eyes, and in the back of their minds, want to swipe you out your seat through the window to have some other girl replace you. With this many options, no one feels just right for each other. There's this anxiety to pass on people because there might always be a better option. So why love at all? Why get married? Why be born for anyone else?

I wrote this rant in my Tinder profile and to my surprise, I was getting fucktons of likes to sift through. I rejected all the artists and led on the writers until I finally picked a blond lawyer with glasses named Gus.

He opened the door of his car for me, the door of the restaurant, and pulled out my chair for me to sit in. When he walked, he stood up straight, exuding confidence. Not the industry kind of confidence but the masculine, strong, quiet kind.

"Have you been here before?" I asked him, referring to the restaurant.

"No. I heard this was the best sushi in town so I had to have you give the final verdict."

"I can't wait."

"Ditto."

That white slip where you check off the rolls you want to order came around and I let him pick first to judge his taste. He ordered yellowtail, albacore, salmon, mackerel, fatty clam, octopus, and eel, the authentic shit. Not wanting to expose my inferior taste, I refused to order the California rolls I wanted, opting for sea urchin, red caviar, and soft-shell crab.

Gus' blue eyes glistened with every tiny gesture, whether he was stirring the ice cubes in his orange soda or squinting whenever he laughed. He was so hot I almost put him on mute when he spoke. There wasn't a shred of anxiety in him. I could ask him a sensitive question and he wouldn't even flinch before answering. He overcame whatever baggage his life dealt him long before meeting me, probably worked it out in some other relationship. Most of the losers I've had crushes on thought their baggage was too complex or special to share. Once they exposed themselves though, their pain sounded completely ordinary, if not boring.

I saved myself for two more dates that only got better and proved Gus wasn't a man-child. As a kisser, he knew how to pick his moments and sync with any rhythm I chose to smooch with. He could lead, follow or switch in between. I was beginning to think he was too good to be true. There had to be one fatal flaw in his character. Perhaps it was hidden beneath his clothes. His hands and feet were big and thick and worn from work. All signs pointed to a real swinger.

He took me to Old Town Pasadena's Masonic Temple for Thursday night's weekly swing dancing. Any kind of physical activity, artistic or not, immediately makes me the center of attention, the girl on two left feet. With Gus leading though, I suddenly seemed to acquire rhythm, poise, and grace.

After breaking a sweat on those glossy planks, jitterbugging to brass sassafras, I knew this would be the night he would finally take me. Making out and feeling each other up on the drive back to my apartment, I didn't bother pretending I wasn't excited. We both were. He passed my test and I gave him every permission.

He parked in front of my building and followed me out the car to my door. After I asked him if he wanted a drink, we started making out until stumbling through my bedroom's portal. His hands caressed my porcelain belly until working their way up onto my ribs, fingers dancing between every groove.

My shirt came off, revealing my white lace bra. He started biting and sucking my nipples through the fabric, sending bolts of pleasure through my body, overriding my nervous system's defensive numbness. He reached around me, kissing my clavicle and unhooked my bra, releasing more flesh for him to play with. He grabbed each big breast in a hand, cupping them to bring up to his lips to kiss, suckle, and nibble. It felt so good I almost came right there but he pulled back when I was mere moments away from eruption.

With fierce dominance, he pulled off my jeans, ringing them around my ankles until I kicked them off completely. Now in only a pair of cream panties, I was a sacred being in a sacred place at a sacred second, too glorious for this world of clothes.

I grabbed his pants and pulled them down, flopping out his hardened cock. As soon as my lips touched his shaft, he melted in front of me with a dire "ugh." He had a perfect cock, stiff, long, solid color, circumcised, clean, tasteful and tasty. Delicate in my mouth and hopefully bold in my pussy. After reaching a hardness I had never seen before, he was ready to penetrate me.

I pulled off my panties and presented my bushy crotch. He smirked as if he could've guessed I was unkempt and began slapping his cock against my clitoris. I began to spasm, my legs locking in unnatural positions. When I thought it was too much to take, he stuck himself inside me giving me nowhere to run. He laid on top of me with the combined force of every activated muscle. I couldn't imagine a more perfect and ethereal sex. This was the sex from Plato's perfect world of forms from which common sex is merely a cheap imitation. He took me in every position, exhausting me until my flesh slacked off the bone. By fuck's end, we laid together, staring up at the ceiling and panting heavily, our minds euphoric messes. Still, 'insatiable-me' recognized something missing.

"How come you didn't eat me out?"

"I dunno, didn't find the right moment. It's too late now, I'm exhausted."

"Are you not into going down on girls?"

"Did I say that?"

"Answer the question."

"No, I'm not."

I reached for my bong on the night cabinet. I packed a bowl in it before I left on our date, anticipating this hit. Sitting up, I burned the weed and inhaled its gaseous cadaver. Exhaling, I passed the bong his way.

"Want some?"

"No, thanks. I don't smoke."

I knew this relationship was doomed before it started but that didn't stop us from dating a whole five months. He would fuck me better than any boy ever had, but if he was too proud to assume the position, he was far from soulmate material. He and I were made of different material altogether.

Without ever telling him, I fashioned a puppet of his likeness, only this puppet was more of a voodoo doll. Using both our hairs, some from his head to enchant the doll, linking it to him then some from my crotch to stuff down the doll's throat, I cursed him into a perpetual state of going down. Whenever I was on my period and we were together, he would have fits of coughing that would put a smile on my face from ear to ear.

Chapter Fifteen

Man

Does writing graphic depictions of sex make me a pervert? Most people, especially men, are addicted to pornography anyway, so why not give them what they're used to? I'm thinking like a manufacturer, not an artist.

Every day I wrote four thousand words and when I'm writing, I'm smoking. Living in that routine, I felt my mental and physical health deteriorate. My lungs and brain blackening at the same rate. After a month, I churned out what I thought would be my first published novel. I called it *Grave-stoned*. The title sounds stupid but the premise was incredibly deep. Death was so prevalent in my life, I imagined and expanded my grief into some kind of worldwide dysphoria, as if the world was simultaneously stoned into grief. In my wish for a cure to my own pain, I set the book's protagonist on a search for a love that would sober the world into happiness. A single pretty pill stuffed with grains of literal angel dust. Our hero's love would trigger the feeling of being in love the world round.

After six rewrites, I sent the manuscript out to every publisher and agent I could find. The rejections came in droves but the pricks of each failure gave me pleasure, not pain. The only times this process hurt was when I didn't hear back from anyone in weeks. A long period of silence met with a rejection email felt as redeeming as a kiss. I sent the manuscript to the San Franciscan and she called me the next day, having spent an entire coke-filled night reading.

"I love it, Ben. You're so talented," she sniffled.

"Really, you mean I'm actually good enough to be a published author?"

"Of course. What kind of a question is that?"

"Then why isn't it happening?"

"Because you don't have any friends in publishing."

"I need friends to be a writer?"

"You need other people to do anything."

"Part of the whole reason I became a writer was because I didn't want to depend on other people."

"Sorry to break the news, honey, but no one is successful by themselves."

"Fuck," I barked.

"Go to a reading. Meet some people. One of them might know somebody."

"So, I have to pretend to be someone's friend and use them for their connections?"

"We all do it. How do you think I became a magician?"

"All right, all right."

"Even if you do get published, you think it'll make you happy? Writers don't make much money, after all."

"It would be a joy no one could ever take away from me."

"That just reeks of naivety."

There was a bookstore a thirty-minute walk away that hosted slews of hipsters on open-mic Wednesdays. It was located in Silverlake, a place where you could buy the best beer of your life but could find nowhere legal to savor it. I arrived at the bookstore before anyone, while they were still setting up the stage. I began looking through the fiction section, pretending I was going to buy something. I scanned through all the covers, realizing I had no interest in books with poorly-designed illustrations. Too many books have covers that give them a B-movie feel, covers that belong in a pharmacy magazine section but had no place beside Henry Miller.

The reading began and the resentment for my fellow writers flowed brilliantly through my veins. They all looked the same or dressed too flamboyantly, conceptually, passing for interesting. The poems, as expected, were drek. Not a unique voice in the flock. They were either too goth, flat, unoriginal, or meaningless. One girl though, that happened to be black, with blacker braids and shades, *set* (as in the opposite of 'shined') below the rest. Every pair of eyes darted between whoever spoke and this charming girl. I quickly jotted something down on my hand and raised it when they asked for the next volunteer. I approached the microphone and stood there for a moment, collecting the anticipation in a Hitlerian way. After twenty seconds of silence, I cleared my throat and began to read off my hand.

"Beautiful woman. With the black skin and blacker braids. I'll buy you a drink."

An upheaval of laughs rang through the room. Her cheeks blushed purple and mine blushed pink. We both smiled at each other, oh so awkwardly.

"I only write haikus. Sorry for interrupting. I'll shut up and sit."

Again, I was laughed to my seat and from there, no one could possibly follow me. The microphone's power was cut to stop anyone from trying. Once everyone stepped out of the bookstore to smoke, I shamelessly eavesdropped on two writers as they pretended not to glance at me out the corners of their eyes.

"My agent has been sending my shit out all over town. Just give it a few days and I'll get a deal."

"Yo, you think I can get that agent's email? Mine isn't returning my calls."

"Sure, man."

"Thank you."

I quickly understood why I wasn't as successful as these writers. Different priorities. The black girl stepped out of the bookstore and I approached her.

"Hey, sorry if I embarrassed you in there."

"Don't be sorry, I thought it was pretty cool."

"Can I buy you that drink?"

"Where do you want to go?"

"I bet you know this area better than I do. I never leave my apartment."

"There's a place down the street."

"I'm following you."

I noticed she had a certain delightful spring in her step that complimented my sluggish bum-foot swagger.

"What's your name?"

"Rocky. You?"

"Ben."

"Rocky and Ben. Okay."

"A Black girl and Jew boy."

She started laughing, "You wanna take it there already?"

"Why not? It's a great mix."

"How do you mean?"

"Ask any interracial love guru. We're worlds apart but still fit together perfectly."

The bar was a novelty dive for low-key high society. We sat down and I ordered us two Pabst Blue Ribbons, the cheapest beer on tap. To people like us it had a charm the craft beers simply couldn't replicate. The nectar of the Gods is great but the piss of the Gods ain't too bad either.

"Did you like the poetry tonight?"

"No, it was terrible," she replied.

"Even mine?"

"At least yours was funny and took courage. That's more indicative of talent than comparing love to spring like that other asshole."

"I wholeheartedly agree. Poetry readings are almost as boring as improv."

"Before we continue, I have to ask you…" she turned to me with a cold look in her eyes, "Do you believe in the existence of a global white supremacist patriarchy?"

I winced and answered "…not really."

"Good. I like you."

We consummated our relationship after a few more dates that were nearly identical to the first. We just drank at this same bar, nothing spontaneous, which was exactly what she wanted. A full-time vacation in leisure world, with no rush or anxiety to be someone you're not. A love too ordinary to ever compare to another. She didn't mind my sexual inadequacy. In fact, to her, I wasn't inadequate at all. Rocky quickly understood my inability to cum during penetration meant I didn't have to use a condom. I told myself I would sooner sever my right hand than lose her.

Chapter Sixteen

Woman

Women have to become independent enough that we can reproduce asexually. By that I mean give birth without requiring semen. It's inevitable. Men are becoming less and less dependable as mates. Male impotence is rising at staggering rates, partly due to pollution and radiation and partly due to pornography which affects the brain similarly to any drug. Sociology is a factor, too. More women are being born and graduating college at higher rates than men. Women are getting better jobs than men. Thus, men are becoming less eligible as mates by not acquiring superior social standing to women. No woman wants a man that is weaker, poorer, and less cool than they are. We don't marry you to be your fucking mothers. A man has to be able to protect his woman and with masculinity being psychologically weened out of men, men cannot even protect themselves. We will be living in the queendom of the Amazons. It sucks but we must prepare for the wave.

~ * ~

Esa and Molly were coming from New York to visit me. They got an Air-BnB Downtown and since I don't have a car, I decided to sleep over while they were here. I tried to tell them Downtown L.A. was just a pastiche of New York but they didn't care. The secluded beaches of Malibu and the Hollywood Hills were the real Los Angeles experience. I walked into the savagely beautiful apartment complex they were staying in and dialed their loft in the callbox.

"Charlotte?"

"Esa?"

"We're ready for you, dear," I heard Molly say.

I made my way to the elevator then was shot up into the sky until stopping level to the heavens. I walked down a hallway to their door and knocked. In the blink of an eye, I was in Esa and Molly's embraces, being rocked back and forth, crying tears of joy.

"I missed you guys so much," I cried.

"We missed you too," Esa cooed.

"I don't have any friends here. I hate everybody. This is the worst city I've ever been to," I blubbered.

"Come back to New York. We could use you. There are jobs waiting for you." They consoled me with kisses.

I pulled away and looked at them.

"If my next relationship sucks, I'll get out of here so fast that the city will forget every trace of me."

"Your next relationship? You need to think more independently, girl," enlightened Esa suggested.

"I know."

We walked into the loft together which had a beautiful blue interior and too many places to sit.

"Look at me, girl, I haven't been in a relationship for two years," Esa said.

"Yeah but wouldn't you want one?"

"Nope. I got this new vibrator, it's NASA technology. Anyone can achieve orgasm anytime, anywhere with this thing. It was even tested in space."

"Speaking of which, I haven't had a tongue down there in forever. My last boyfriend would've rather sucked his own."

"Men are pigs. They can't stay hard without us blowing them but returning the favor is somehow extra? What the fuck is that?" Esa said.

"*Mhmm*," I replied.

We spent the night the same way we would've in college. Smoking weed, eating takeout, and watching movies.

"After the movie, ya'll want to get a drink?"

"Why?" Esa asked.

"I don't know, maybe we could meet some guys."

"I'm already tired," Esa shrugged.

"I'd be down, Charlotte," Molly nodded.

"Cool," I replied.

Esa sighed. "Well, I guess I'm in."

The film faded to black and we wiped away our tears, slowly gathering ourselves before a heavy, collective yawn that shot us up off the couch. Treading into LA's tribute diorama knock-off of New York's historic Broadway Ave, we found a bar we felt something might happen in and numerous vodka cocktails deep, we recanted tales of our youth. You might think we're still young, but to us, youth faded the moment we were crushed by the responsibility of a day job.

"Did you ever see or talk to that one Jewish guy you were in love with senior year?"

"No. he doesn't have Facebook or Instagram or anything. I don't know how I'd find him."

"You're not trying to, are you?"

"No, but he's from Los Angeles, so it's possible I could run into him."

"Damn, you're still thinking about him," Esa bemoaned. "That bastard."

Vodka was the most 'fun drunk' we knew, as exemplified by Molly getting up onto the bar and dancing the *cha cha cha* when The Smiths shuffled over the jukebox. The bouncer had to pull her down and she fell into his bulky brown arms. After trying to plant a few smooches on him, he threw her out of the bar. Alone out there, Molly waited for us while Esa and I went to the bathroom to piss, marking our territory. After finishing and washing our hands together, I noticed Esa looking at me rather oddly.

"What's wrong?"

Esa went in for a kiss. I was shocked but acted instantly. I pulled back, not because I wasn't open to experimenting but because she hadn't earned it.

"What the fuck!?"

I pushed her away and she shook her head, pretending to snap out of a trance.

"Sorry, fuck. I'm so toasted. I don't know what came over me. Molly told you I came out the closet, right?"

"No...she didn't tell you I did, right? Because if she did then she fucking lied."

"I just felt for some reason you needed..."

"Needed what?"

"What a woman could give you."

"I am a woman. I can give it to myself."

"You know what, forget it. Let's just go outside."

Outside, Molly was in the midst of making out with a stranger. They held their cigarettes out, letting them burn. I could see his eyes soberly scanning through the slits of his lids at his drunken victim. Esa and I pulled Molly away from him, disrupting his dream.

"What the fuck?" he bitched.

"Sorry, man but we gotta go," Esa shouted.

"Thanks for the cigarette, bro," Molly laughed, having already forgotten the kiss' meaning.

"You might want to think about getting different friends, girl. Fuckin' cockblocks."

Laughing together, we careened down the cold concrete toward whatever bar would be dumb enough to host us. The open street warped into a spinning hallway.

"Here that? You guys are cockblocks. Why'd you have to block my cock?" Molly slurred, laughing so hard she almost heaved.

Seeing Molly almost vomit sent all the malicious take-out Vietnamese food back up Esa's throat. She started puking into a gutter outside a bar and we found ourselves stuck by her side, stroking her back.

"I'm sorry. I knew I shouldn't have gone out tonight."

"Don't worry about us, girl. Just let it all out. Tomorrow we'll wake up at three and forget any of this shit ever happened.

She threw up a few more gritty bits before turning to me with glistening, grey lips and eyes.

"Forgive me, Charlotte. For what I did earlier."

"What happened?" Molly asked.

"Nothing, it was stupid. Not even a big deal," I answered.

"I just want you to get over that guy," Esa continued.

"Which guy?"

"From college."

"It's been years. I'm over him."

"I don't think you are. I think it's fucked with you ever since."

"Would you ever date a guy that rejected you? No, right, well I definitely wouldn't."

"Then it's not him you want, it's revenge."

"Shut up, you don't know what you're talking about, you sloppy bitch."

What a shame after all this time spent away from each other, the first night we go out and we're already at each other's throats. I couldn't stand sleeping in the same loft as Esa that night so after I walked them back, I got an Uber and took it all the way home where I curled up into bed with Jinx. Alone with my cat, the one thought that crossed my drunken mind was Ben. Really anytime I went out for the night into the city's heart, I had some strange mix of hope and anxiety I'd see him again. I don't know what I'd say if I did, I imagine it would be incredibly awkward but the idea of seeing him feels like some necessary rite of passage. Until that happens, I don't think I'll be able to love anyone as truly myself.

Chapter Seventeen

Man

Rocky and I had been working on our poetry for days, perfecting a few sonnets for an upcoming open mic. She had a spellbinding voice, not in its sound but in its originality. After we'd make love, she would ask me to tell her a story. I'd improvise characters, settings, and plots off the top of my head as naturally as a stream flows. We made grand plans for our future, imagining our bi-racial children and what forms of entertainment they would pursue. She even read my novel and edited it so when I sent it out for a second time, I actually got a few publishing offers back. I didn't accept any of them because their contracts seemed shady, their business licenses were expired, or they only offered to publish for e-book. Rocky told me to wait for a deal that would get my books distributed to mainstream bookstores. She thought I was incredible. Every time she praised my talent, I reminded her it was our teamwork that made the writing shine.

The other night in bed she asked me, "Have you ever been in love?"

"Nope. What about you?"

"Numerous times."

"I guess we have different definitions of love."

"What's yours?"

"Lifelong commitment."

"Is that why you haven't told me you love me?"

"Yes."

"Well, have you ever felt what you feel for me for anyone else?"

"No. Every person gets their own feeling."

"Ugh, you had to have felt something for someone."

"I have, just not love and not what I feel for you."

"Then who, what did you feel for them?"

"There was this girl. In college."

"What was her name? What was she like?"

"We had a painting class together. Her name was Charlotte."

"How long were you guys dating?"

"We didn't date at all."

"Then how did you feel anything for her?"

"My feelings were unrequited…"

"Oh, I'm sorry."

"Don't be…I'm bullshitting. Sorry. Really, her feelings were unrequited."

"You rejected her?"

"I didn't let myself accept her."

"You regret it."

I looked at Rocky with tired eyes.

"It's okay. I understand. Why didn't you let yourself love?"

"My mind took total control of my life."

"What does that mean? Your mind is always in control."

"No, the mind is supposed to listen to the demands of the body. I let it take control and almost lost myself."

"You went crazy?"

"I've been crazy for a very long time. Either I've been hiding it well since I started dating you or somehow you killed it."

"I killed the crazy?"

I nodded and smiled.

We woke up the next morning and I could tell she hadn't forgotten about the girl I once obsessed over. She made coffee and set a cup of it on a thin china plate beside the bed. On the plate were also two cigarettes for us to enjoy in bed. She jumped over my gut and laid on the other side of me while I took the coffee and rested it on my chest so she could reach it. She took one of the cigarettes and lit it. I put the coffee up to my lip but before I took a sip, I looked at her, noticing a quiet resentment in her cold expression.

"What's wrong?"

"I think you're still in love with that girl."

"I very explicitly told you I've never been in love."

"You were just too chickenshit to love her. You'd probably rather take a time machine and go back to her than stay in the present with me."

"You really are a brilliant writer because no normal person could ever imagine anything that absurd."

"Just because it's absurd doesn't mean it's untrue."

"But it *is* untrue."

"I think you don't know your own heart. You clearly felt something for this girl but you acted like you didn't. You lied to yourself. Maybe you're lying to yourself right now. So, then you're lying to me too."

"I make a point to be honest with myself and you all the time."

"What's her name?"

"I told you."

"What's her last name? Charlotte what?" She drew her phone like a pistol, ready to sniff the competition out on the internet.

"I'm not going to tell you."

"Why not? What are you afraid of?"

"Maybe you should go, I need to write."

"*Oh?* I thought we were a team."

"Rocky. Please, put out that cigarette and go." I raised my voice.

She took her cigarette and crushed it into my shoulder. I could feel the tissue melt into liquid and cool into the new shape of a wound. I jumped and the coffee resting on my chest jumped with me, scalding me with a rain of shocking pain. Blood coursed through my heart and adrenaline rushed through my brain as both organs throbbed against the bone. I stood up, grabbed Rocky, dragged her off the bed and pushed her out the door. I left her standing there, in the hallway, wearing nothing but her shirt and panties.

"You're really going to let me stand out here half-naked?"

I reopened the door to throw her clothes in her face then slammed it back closed without a care for where she'd go. It's a good thing I never told her I loved her. I was proud of my restraint. This was the first real fight I ever had with a girlfriend. I was proud of that too.

Chapter Eighteen

Woman

My evenings after work were spent making puppets for a grand show I imagined in my mind. I had written a play about two puppets in a woman's prison talking about their husbands. They end up seducing each other in a very animated panic I intended to perform live. The hand puppets, Muffy and Tumble, were two fuzzy blue cuties that looked like they hadn't gotten laid in years.

The night of the open mic, I scampered over to this Silverlake bookstore with my cardboard box home for puppets. Arriving early, one of the first people there, when they asked for volunteers from the modest audience, my hand shot up and I was picked to perform first. I got up on stage, set down my box and fit Muffy and Tumble onto each of my hands. Having mastered ventriloquism over the last couple of years, the puppets spoke in two different voices coming from a small opening in my shut lips.

"Girl, if it wasn't for my feminist theory class, I think I'd go crazy in the pen."

"Really, what kind of stuff are you learning?"

"Let me show you."

The puppets started making out and slowly, Tumble removed Muffy's shirt. Just then, through the door in the back of the store, strode in Ben Weiss with some girl I could only assume was his wife. The entire performance seemed to pause for a crude beat as my eyes fixed upon them then quickly returned to task. I could feel myself sweating as I was sure they were both staring at me. I needed to examine his reaction so I looked up again and saw him casually wave. The performance was going downhill fast. To see what caught my attention, the entire audience was staring back at Ben. With their eyes diverted from me, I slipped off my puppets, threw them back into their box, picked it up and made a break for the exit. Without a word, the performance was over. Storming up the street, I could hear the soft hum of laughter from inside of the store. The moment I asked for miraculously came but I couldn't even find the balls to grab it. I was too cowardly to deserve it. If I just stayed put and spoke to Ben after the show, confidently asking him out for coffee in front of that bitch he was with, maybe something could've happened.

~ * ~

That night, the only thing that could turn my heartache into harmless static was my phone, which occupied me until dawn. At six a.m. I got an Instagram message from a profile calling themselves BenWeiss1.

It was good seeing you last night. Wish we could've talked.

I felt my heart flush into my fingers. Once I forced myself to accept the lackluster of our first words together being over text and not in person, I began typing with frantic enthusiasm.

I still can't believe you were there.

I wish you finished your show.

I was too embarrassed. It wasn't ready yet. That's why I left.

Oh good. I thought it was because of me.

As if.

Do you want to get coffee sometime, maybe catch up?

I had to pinch myself. Ben Weiss was asking me out.

Did you make this profile just to message me? At six a.m.?

What makes you think that?

You have no followers or pictures.

Okay, yeah, I did. I don't use social media and I wanted to talk to you.

Who was that girl you were with?

My ex.

You still hang out?

We broke up last night because she was jealous of you...so how about that coffee? he asked again.

Sure. Meet me in North Hollywood at the Starbucks on Magnolia and Lankershim at eight p.m.

I'll see you there.

I didn't respond and he deleted his profile only minutes later.

I arrived at Starbucks at seven forty-five p.m., hoping to be early enough to see him coming but he was already there.

"How long have you been here?"

"Ten minutes."

He held his arms out to hug me and when I fell into them, I could feel a warming nervousness through his coat. When he pulled away, we both found our seats at a table.

"Can we sit outside so I can smoke?"

"Sure."

We got right up and left the Starbucks.

"Actually, are you hungry?" I asked.

"Sure," he replied.

"There's a good ramen place I know around here."

He nodded and lit up a cigarette and we abandoned any interest in corporate coffee.

"Why did you want to see me again?"

"Because I consider us friends in a weird way. I remember you fondly when I think of you."

"You still think of me? We only had one class together."

"I was in a weird phase of my life at that time. Weird but important to me."

"Is it me you remember or a time in your life when I was an extra?"

"It's you."

"Fair enough."

I opened the door of the ramen restaurant for myself and we were seated immediately. Things were quiet at first. We tried not to make it so obvious we were checking each other out. A few wrinkles were setting in on his face and a grey hair or two peppered his black curls.

"So, what do you do now?"

"I guess I'm a journalist. That's what I get paid for."

"Good. You ended up a writer."

"I'm glad you remember, but a journalist isn't a writer. No matter how much they want to be. I do novels too, as always. When one gets published, then I'll be a writer. Are you making puppets?"

"For a really stupid TV show."

"Which one?"

"*Hamburger Hotdog.*"

"Love that show."

"Shut up," I laughed.

We both ordered the vegetable ramen and a tasty Japanese beer to share. I was wondering who would bring up college first until finally deciding it had to be me.

"So why were you so antisocial in college?"

"Hopefully this doesn't sound weird...I thought if I wanted to be a writer, I had to sacrifice being social. I thought being totally alone would make me the best."

"Did it work?"

"Probably not. Other people would've given me more insight into life. The upside was that isolation let writing take up all my time."

"Do you have time for people now?"

"When I started dating Rocky, I was thirty thousand words into a new book. Today I'm thirty-one thousand words in. In three months, I've only written a thousand words. I need someone who knows how to leave me alone."

"Shouldn't be too hard to find."

"Are you dating anyone?"

"I was a few months ago. He was perfect on the surface but upon closer inspection, he was the biggest douchebag I have ever known."

There was a long pause. Maybe he was trying to stomach the thought of another man having me the way he thought he should.

"Are we shallow people?"

"Everyone is on some level but who cares? We're just as worthy of happiness as anyone."

"Cheers to that."

He raised his glass and met mine. Their clinking together rang through my head with the echo of bells. We split the bill and cruised out the restaurant. I quietly ordered an Uber for myself then watched him mill about the street, his hands in his pockets, his eyes on his feet.

"Do you want to do this again?"

He quickly looked up at me.

"You still owe me a movie or a jazz show."

He smiled. "This time I won't be weird."

"I doubt it but you can try."

"Did you drive here?"

"No. I don't do that."

"How can you not drive? You've lived in L.A. your whole life."

"I know how, I just don't want any unnecessary expenses. I wouldn't be able to support myself writing if I had car and insurance payments to worry about."

"Yeah, I never learned how but if I did, I'm sure I'd do the same."

Suddenly, the Uber pulled up and I hugged Ben goodbye. I got inside and watched him vanish as the driver turned a corner. At that moment, a sharp fear hit me. It was a sense of distrust. At any moment, he could withdraw and let me down. That was his style, somewhere between cowardly and mystery. He'd rather be puzzled over than present.

Chapter Nineteen

Man

I decided I would walk home, all the way from North to East Hollywood. Using my sense of memory as a map, I was totally unsure of where I was going. This was actually my favorite thing to do in Los Angeles, fade into the night's landscape and become an insignificant witness to the giant swarm of cars, their lights streaking. By the time I reached my apartment, nearly three hours later, the soles of my feet felt like they had been grated off. All I had was this familiar feeling of either love or infatuation and no way to tell them apart. Literary genius is poisoned by love. I already knew this but seeing Charlotte reaffirmed it. The decision in front of me was now to write or to love and very foolishly, I chose to love her.

Not texting for a few days was the custom in Los Angeles. You had to pretend other girls were speaking to you and occupying so much of your time you couldn't communicate in a respectful manner. Dishonesty is the nature of dating and jealousy is gravity in the city of angels. That is what good women want, someone in demand, someone who will choose them over another girl. So, in a sense Rocky did me a solid by giving Charlotte the impression I was eligible.

Talking about men and women in these terms does not give me some chauvinistic kick. My understanding of the genders is based in biology. Looking at nature, the masculine and feminine aspects express themselves even in flowers, where in order to reach the feminine ovary, the masculine pollen must pass the test of a long style in the flower's center. The pollen wants to seed and spread as much as possible while the ovary prudishly denies any unworthy suitor.

The standard waiting period of three days had past and I was free to text her. Like a clever boy, I figured I wouldn't waste her time with a plebian 'what's up, how are you?' I wanted to show her I knew how to have fun with words.

As transcendent as that ramen was, wait till you hear the jazz I plan to take you to.

Can you believe I actually wrote that? 'Transcendent'? Who do I think I am? Some people are so smart they're stupid. I didn't deserve a reply and I didn't get one. I'm sure she was either creeped out by my eagerness, switched gears onto someone else after reading that text, or wanted me to suffer through the silent treatment. My nights without an answer were met with incredible hemorrhaging from the heart. It was a shrinking and stupefying detachment from all planes of reality until I became a new dimension unto myself.

When I schizophrenically cracked into a daze of half-sleep, my brain wrung out a terrible nightmare. I was riding a white horse through golden clouds. Kamadeva, the Hindu equivalent of Cupid, rode up beside me on his bird. He grabbed his bow and reached over his shoulder, into his holster and in between each of his fingers, drew a different arrow. Kamadeva's arrows were named the Inflamer, the Parcher, the Infatuator, the Inciter of the Paroxysm of Desire, and the Carrier of Death. Pulling all five arrows back into his bow and aiming at me, he landed all five in my head, sending me flying off my horse, through the clouds, back down to my bed, where I woke up. Three days later, during what must have been her lunch hour from work, Charlotte finally texted back.

Hey, sorry. I'm just reading this now. Sure, just let me know when the show is and I'll see you there.

Her intentions were laid out clearly in this text. She would've rather met me there than shared a ride and thus didn't consider me a romantic prospect. Had I not been deranged by the pain I felt, perhaps I could've understood the text for what it was and not attributed my own delusion to it. That delusion being that I was being tested by the world to see if I could win Charlotte and that I ultimately deserved her as a reward for overcoming the calamities I had been through in my life. I took this text as her playing hard to get but really, she wasn't even playing.

Awesome. Meet me at the Blue Whale at eight p.m. on Saturday. I hope you like hard piano.

I love hard piano, she replied an hour later.

I'd see a reply like that and convince myself she was sending me mixed signals. If she loved something I suggested, like hard piano, then she could eventually love me. That Saturday Mark Herman was performing his entire album "The Pained Piano" at the Blue Whale.

Herman's black piano stood in the center of a circle as numerous romantically placed and set tables sat around the artist, occupied by couples passing back and forth tiny gestures of true love. Between each note was the silence of love unquestioned and after each song were the murmurs of love affirmed. Yet when Charlotte arrived twenty minutes late and sat beside me, her apology rang with an offsetting sentiment. I looked around the room. Everyone but us was in love. All I could do was charge my glances with thoughts of tender reverence but still she couldn't read me. I already saw my failure ahead but stubbornly rejected the signs that foreshadowed it.

"Are you enjoying this?" I asked.

"Yeah. Sorry, it's been a long day."

Apart from that, we were silent and by the time the show was finished, it was so late that we didn't have enough time to be ourselves around each other.

"Would you like to get one more drink before you go?"

"No thanks, I don't feel like getting drunk. The show was nice, though. Thanks for inviting me."

"No problem…I feel like we barely spoke tonight."

"What did you expect? It's a concert," she laughed.

I shrugged. "I guess you're right. Want to check out a movie next time?"

"To talk during the movie?" She laughed again.

"You're right, sorry. I dunno, how about dinner then?"

"I'll let you know," she answered, like a knife through my heart.

We hugged before she hopped into an Uber and left. The pain only grew the closer I got to her because the more time we spent together, the more obvious it was we weren't going to start dating. It was a sad roll of the dice. The gods didn't see the beauty in the story I wanted written for Charlotte and me. They had their own plans as to how our lives should go. I knew the forces that controlled this world were heartless but I didn't realize they were this fucking stupid.

Chapter Twenty

Woman

As crazy as it sounds, as badly as my friends would want to kick my ass for thinking it, after all these years, I still feel like I could fall in love with Ben. I should've known better than to question my clairvoyance in the first place. Love takes time. In our case, years to develop and bloom. That doesn't mean he wouldn't have to earn my love though. I'd sooner defy my own destiny than let him have me without a fight. It's not that I wanted to see him struggle, it's that Ben had to win over my heart, which he hasn't done by any measure. It takes more than my understanding that he will be loyal and devoted to me. He has to seduce me and make me feel like every moment we share together is new, special, and far from ordinary.

The day after our date at the Blue Whale, I woke up that Sunday morning to an unexpected knock at my door. I looked through the peephole and saw a delivery boy holding a big bouquet of red roses on the other side. When I opened the door, he handed the roses to me, tipped his hat with a smile, and left me to read the tag attached. It simply read, *From your secret admirer*. It was a bit corny but intriguing. Ben was the thoughtful sort but this wasn't him. I wouldn't be surprised if this came from some stranger who saw me walk to the corner market for brunch one time and took a fancy to my legs. Smarter girls wouldn't want to pry into the unknown, seeing as the unknown could mean a slit throat the way people are in this time and town. I was open to anything, though. I set the roses in a vase upon my windowsill and for days, the passing glance I'd give them served as a constant reminder there were always other boys. The next text I received from Ben was a sad attempt to impress me.

I got us two tickets to the premiere of the new Terrence Malick film.
I was neither a fan of Malick, nor interested in seeing a movie with Ben for our third outing. Not to mention, the tickets were open to the public, so it's not like he got us into some private Hollywood red carpet. I didn't want to say no though, not yet at least. That same day, after my lunch break, I went into the employee's lounge at the studio and saw a puppet sitting on the table with a bright gold ribbon wrapped around it. The puppet was a unicorn with a horn of rainbow stripes. I approached the magical creature with my hand out as if to let it know I was friendly, a hand I planned on inserting into its bum. Once my hand fit inside it and I pulled off the ribbon, I read a message written on the tag attached to the unicorn's back.

I've narrowed down the field of possible people I could be. You now know we work together. The thing that made me realize you were special was your incredible ethic and talent when it comes to playing with puppets. I made this unicorn for you, Charlotte, because you're just as unique.

My heart sank with a lovely swoon despite all my efforts to pull it back into place and maintain the hope Ben will wake up one day, knowing how to win me. There was nothing I could do though, my mind wanted Ben but the rest of my body began falling for this mystery man. And at the end of the day, the mind must serve the body. I strolled around set with the unicorn trying to judge by everyone's reactions who the culprit creator could've been. The production assistants seemed totally oblivious. The grips were smoking and sneaking in swigs of booze without a care for anyone but the wolf pack. My fellow puppeteers were all too nerdy to desire me or for me to desire. The actors were too self-obsessed to even remember my name then I saw our director, Brad. He sat in his director's chair wearing a unicorn T-shirt. He smiled at me and suddenly, it felt like I was walking toward him against my own accord.

"Nice puppet."

"Nice shirt."

"Did you do this?"

He nodded.

"The roses too?"

"Were they beautiful?"

I nodded.

"Good."

"I don't know what to say."

"Will you get dinner with me tonight?"

"Yes."

"Cool. I'll pick you up at seven."

I stood around not knowing where to go until the assistant director swung around and told us to get ready for rehearsal in five. I slowly walked backward to my position and with one last glance at him, I saw Brad confidently wink. The rest of the day, my heart was racing and my mind was elsewhere. I messed up cues and needed to smoke a cigarette during break which I never do. Just shy of seven, Brad pulled up to my apartment in a black BMW and we zipped away into the night.

He took me to Beverly Hills, for my first proper dinner in Los Angeles, the way this city's creators intended meals to be eaten. Gentle music, wine, and penetrating ambiance won me over before we even got our food. The only issue with Brad was that he was ten years older than me, which in hindsight does make it seem weird that a guy in his late thirties would go through the trouble of becoming my secret admirer. I didn't care though. I'll sacrifice the romantic authenticity of dating someone the same age for money. It's not like Brad made his fortune banking. He was an artist just like me.

When the date of Terrence Malick's premiere came around, I told Ben I was sick and staying in for the night. Dishonesty is not a sin but is actually a necessary tactic for survival in a woman's life. I spent the night with Brad, enjoying wine and weed at his Venice beach boardwalk house. We would listen to the waves roll in as he would rub my feet and legs and not for a second did any other person, place, or thing cross my mind. I felt on the edge of some marvelous fall into the pleasurable unknown. We made love for the first time that night and I could feel the difference in the rhythm he fucked with compared to a younger man. He wasn't as able to control himself and his body began to lock up under the overwhelming pleasure of my sex.

"I'm sorry."

He pulled out but I could still feel him in me.

"Damn it, I knew you should've worn a condom."

"Little too late now," he said after rolling off of me.

"What am I going to do if I get pregnant?"

"You won't."

"How do you know?"

"I just do and if I'm wrong, we'll figure it out."

After washing up, I lay still and silent for about twenty minutes thinking about my future. Even though I was dead set on being a puppeteer and an independent woman, I had already started feeling the urge to have a child. To take care of someone or something. I had Jinx but Jinx never needed me like a child needs its mother. If I were to wait much longer, into my thirties, I'd be met with multitudes of unsuccessful men still searching for partners, desperately trying to get married and start families with whoever was dumb enough to shuck away their lives to them.

I always knew I'd be a good mother too. My child would be my world and I'd sacrifice everything for him. I will have a son. I've already foreseen it. I will raise him to be a fighter. He will have to be one. With the end of civilization drawing near, not only will he need to be strong, but so will I. The souls of our children visit us before they are born. If Brad does indeed get me pregnant then our son's soul is already in this room, swimming above our heads.

My birthday was coming up soon and I still hadn't gone out with Ben since the Blue Whale. Every time he would ask me out, I would either ignore his text or tell him I was busy. It seemed the more I shit on him, the more frequently he would ask. For my birthday, even though I was already Brad's girlfriend, I felt sorry for Ben and invited him. We reserved a table and bottle service at Zone, one of Los Angeles' best hip-hop clubs and Brad didn't even flinch at the prospect of covering the bill. That night of my Sagittarian celebration, a bunch of us took a limo to the club and once we arrived, we walked right past the long line and bouncer. The trap music was buzzing through the air as we sang rowdily around our table and had Brad make cocktails for us all. Maybe an hour into the night, after I already danced into a sweat, Ben finally got into the club, looking too disheveled to fit in with our company. He got to our table and quickly saw every seat was taken, forcing him to stand and just stare at me, the only person he knew. Brad made some comment about Ben to me that I pretended to hear but couldn't over the music. He then started laughing and I followed in step, making Ben visibly embarrassed. Ben then did something that was totally out of character. He made himself a drink, took one sip, and poured the rest over Brad's head. Brad instantly jumped at him, rabid, wanting to fight but security got in between them, escorting Ben out. Brad tried to follow them but I grabbed him, refusing to let go.

"You're staying right here."

"What the fuck? Did you see what that asshole did to me in front of all our friends?"

"I don't care. If you go out there right now, we're through."

Brad let out a heavy sigh, settled down and went to the bathroom to wash up. When he came back, I saw the knuckles on his right hand were bruised. I figured I wouldn't speak to Ben again unless he wanted to apologize, which I doubt he would. The following day, I bought a pregnancy test for the first time in my life and took the test at Brad's house. I pissed over the white stick and when the result appeared, my heart started bouncing around like a pinball inside my chest.

"It came out positive."

I heard Brad's sneakers skid on the floor as he ran over to me. He pushed open the locked bathroom door and stuck his head in.

"You're pregnant?"

I jumped up off the toilet and wrapped my arms around him.

"Yes."

He picked me up, spun me around, set me down and kissed me.

"So, you're happy?" I asked.

It took him a moment. Hesitating, he answered, "Sure."

"Sure? What do you mean, sure?"

"I mean, yeah. This is awesome."

I took my hands off of him and he took his off of mine. I didn't even need to ask him if he meant it. He knew I knew he didn't.

"Come on, babe, this is life-changing news. Don't expect me to know how to feel right away."

"I don't know why I was so ecstatic." I hung my head and wallowed out of the bathroom, feeling like shit.

"It was an accident, Charlotte. You can't deny that."

I glared at him angrily, like a defensive mother. "You really need to learn what thoughts to keep to yourself, Brad."

Chapter Twenty-One

Man

Heartache has always been the only condition that inspired me to create good literature. Sometimes, I think I subconsciously go looking for it whenever I go long enough without having written anything of substance.

I actually cried walking home from Charlotte's party and everyone on that packed Hollywood boulevard sidewalk laughed at me. That pain persisted for days until I sat down in front of my computer, feeling ready to write something. Then as Microsoft Word loaded up, I got a phone call from none other than my brother, Jerry.

"Hey Ben."

"*Jerry?*"

"That's right, Ben. Can you guess why I'm calling you?"

"Is Dad sick?"

"God forbid…what's wrong with you? No. I'm calling you because I'll be in Los Angeles next week."

"Really? How long have you known you were coming here?"

"I met a girl from L.A. last month on an app. Anyway, we're in love now and I have to go to Los Angeles to see her."

"Cool, so it sounds like you'll be too busy with her to see me. Don't worry though, I won't take it personally if we don't hang out."

"Hang on…she has a job. If you don't mind, since I know you have all this free time, can you show me around L.A. while she's at work?"

"How do you know I have free time?"

"You're a writer."

"Yeah, that's a job."

"No, it's not."

I rolled my eyes.

"Call me when you're in L.A. Maybe I'll have time for you...*maybe*."

"I know you're joking so I'm not going to be pissed...*dickhead*."

Jerry hung up the phone. I stared at the keyboard. The computer screen, my fingers and the flickering vertical line on Microsoft Word were begging me to type. I was ready to prove my genius only minutes before but now I was stuck in neutral.

Jerry arrived in Los Angeles and his girl picked him up from the airport. He stayed with her for a few days and didn't bother calling me until Wednesday night, just three days after he arrived, at eleven thirty p.m. His ring startled me awake and I answered the phone, frustrated to no end.

"Fuckin aye, Jerry."

"What?"

"It's eleven thirty, man."

"How old are you, bro? Fucking eighty?"

"What do you want?"

"The bitch kicked me out of her place."

"What?"

"I need to come over."

"You're not coming here."

"I need to see you, Ben. I need someone now. I'm not okay."

We always joked around so much when things took a serious turn, we couldn't even recognize it without one of us making it clear. My flesh and blood actually needed me. This moment might never happen again, especially if I chose to be selfish.

"I'll text you my address. Uber here."

"Thanks, Ben. I'll see you soon."

He arrived fifteen minutes later, coming out of the Uber with a duffel bag of clothes. He held his arms out to hug me and we did for the first time since our Mother died. We held each other until he started sobbing on my shoulder. I felt the instinct to complain bubble up in me but suppressed it and wisely chose to sympathize.

"There, there, Jerry. At least you got laid."

"I was in fucking love with this girl and she tore my heart out."

"Didn't you only meet her online a month ago?"

"She said she loved me and wanted to be with me forever." He pulled away and looked at me. I had never seen my superior so weakened and destroyed.

"Look, you're still young. There are plenty of women that would love to be with you. Women living where you live. Real ones, not digital."

"I'm thirty fucking six, Ben. Every respectable person around me is already married...*why doesn't anybody want me?*"

"I know how it feels, Jerry. I fell deeply in love with a girl, now she fucking hates me and I still fucking love her. She shits on me and I'm obsessed with her. She makes me hate myself and it's fucking killing me every night out here."

Some switch in Jerry's brain flipped on and suddenly he became my older brother again, forgetting his own heartbreak to remedy mine.

"Come on, Ben."

He started walking down the street and waved me over.

"Where are we going?"

"To get a drink...or three."

Our tears dried quickly as we romped around the cold Los Angeles night. We bought a six pack of shit beer and six mini-shots of tequila from a liquor store then ducked out into an alleyway to drink. With every beer, we took a shot, imagining this alley were some boxcar bar that we had all to ourselves.

"I remember one time you said hell and heaven are states of mind. I think I finally know what you meant."

"You feel like you're in hell right now?"

"I know it."

"You're not, Jerry."

"Really? If I'm not then who is?"

I pointed to a bum at the other end of the alley. He was trying to bite his own ear off with dried blue froth in the corners of his crusted lips. Between bites, he'd "baa" like a goat. It was a sight too crazed to turn away from or acknowledge amidst polite company.

"That guy right there. He's in hell. You're not. Not today."

Jerry took his beer bottle and threw it at the bum. It shattered in a loud crash right at his feet. The bum then yipped and skittered away on all fours, still scared for his miserable life.

"That's right. Get the fuck out of here. This is our alley now."

Jerry took the last beer, which was meant for me, and pulled his arm back to throw it like a football. I grabbed him with all my might, trying to save my last cold one.

"What the fuck's wrong with you, Jerry!?"

"I need to break something or hurt someone. If I don't, I'm just going to fucking explode."

"You want to hurt someone? Hurt me, bro."

"You feel like getting crushed tonight, baby bro?" he said, testing me.

Jerry pushed me away but I was able to pry the beer out of his hand. I popped off the cap, took a huge swig then threw the half-empty bottle against the wall. Its shattering empowered me, pumping me up.

"Tonight's as good a night as any. Try me, motherfucker," I challenged him.

I took off my shirt and threw it aside, revealing my slinky white body.

"Get some."

Jerry came at me and immediately got me into a noogie, grating his knuckles into my skull. I started pounding him with a barrage of punches to his gut that he absorbed with no sign of pain other than a rigid smile on his face.

"That all you got, baby bro?"

"Fuck you."

"Awwww, you're adorable but you gotta mind your fucking manners."

He spun me out of his noogie and I stumbled backward. Jerry then did a jumping dragon kick that caught me right in the dick. I fell to my knees, groaning, all systems scrambling, my nuts shooting up into my stomach.

"Sorry, Ben, I meant to hit your face."

My knees fell to the cold concrete and puked up a little puddle.

"It's all good," I winced. "Just give me a minute and I'll take you to a motel."

"You don't want to get another six pack first?"

"Sure. Hang on. My nuts are throbbing."

"I never wanted to be an uncle anyway."

Chapter Twenty-Two

Woman

If you would've told me what Los Angeles had in store for me, I would've never left New York. I was now ten weeks pregnant and started to show. I was eating for two and ballooning into a healthy white peach. Every morning saw me puke up a little food and my whole body would surge with heat and pain. Brad was still in the picture but the love was gone. We stopped having sex and he became less present once he realized how much we needed him. I felt it would be better to stay with my mom, but when I asked her if I could come home, she booked a flight to Los Angeles to come stay with me. Her company only alienated Brad more, making him feel like he was forced into our weird family.

"He won't stay around," my mother warned me one night while Brad was out with friends and we were eating ice cream, watching conservative cable news.

"Brad's a good man, Mom. He'll be there for us."

"Has he asked to marry you?"

"No."

"He won't, dear."

"You don't know that."

"Charlotte, I've been around a long time. You're just like me. Men like your father or this asshole come into a girl's life and the girl can't see the bastards for who they really are."

"Brad reminds you of my father?"

"Only in that both men didn't want us. You'd have been better off with a man that was a boring, safe bet but now it's too late. With a child, no man will want you."

"I thought the rich guy was the safe bet."

"The safe bet is the one that loves you more than anything in the world."

I sat quietly thinking of Ben in a solemn moment of reflection. I didn't regret not choosing him, though there's no reason I should believe he would've been able to take care of me even if he wanted.

"A poor boy that loves you is better than a rich one that doesn't. Love will make him do anything to take care of his woman. Even if it breaks his back, love will make him find a way," my mother assured me.

That night I had a dream. I woke up in my Brooklyn bedroom and saw a wondrous snowfall of white feathers outside my window. I crawled out of bed, then through the window to watch from the fire escape. Out on the railing, Jinx was huddled over something, trying to hide it from me. I pushed him away to find a rat's corpse and a screwdriver with a bloody tip. I assumed it was the rat's blood on the tip and got so scared that I tripped over the railing. Instead of falling to my death, I sprouted wings out of my pregnant belly and began soaring over the city. I glided with unparalleled freedom, watching everyone happily getting on with their lonely lives until the feathers of my wings fell off, dwindling down to the raw skin. I plummeted to the ground and woke up to the sound of my mother snoring as she slept on the love seat. Something about the dream tranquilized my stomach and for the first time in a long while, I didn't wake up feeling nauseous.

The weather was perfect to go to the beach. Brad was supposed to arrive at ten a.m. to take us but wasn't answering his phone. Once it was obvious he wasn't coming, my mother made a late breakfast for two and I spent the rest of the day waiting on his call until the hours wasted away into the night. The emotional pain inspired a physical reaction and when I stood up off the couch there was a brand-new ache in my back. An ache that sent a metallic taste in my mouth with every step. I groaned on my way to the fridge as I got my favorite bucket of mint chip ice cream. When I sat back down on the couch, my mother changed the channel to cable news where they were covering the president's historic meeting with the prime minister of North Korea. It was the first time the olive branch had been extended to the isolated nation, and if anything would make people falsely believe in hope for this world it was this.

"Can you believe it? Earth is a more peaceful place today than it was yesterday," my mother said.

"There's nothing in the treaty that makes either nation less of a threat."

"But we're friends now. It's a step in the right direction."

"Leaders like to deceive each other. That's all this is. The real question is which party will break their promises first."

"Always such a pessimist. Maybe if you were a happier person Brad would be here right now."

"Don't make me throw this ice cream at your head."

"Why isn't he here?"

"I don't know, maybe he didn't want to be around you."

"What's wrong with me?"

"You're bossy, selfish, and annoying, Mom...I could go on if you want."

"At least I give a shit. Unlike him."

I grit my teeth, got up and went to sleep early to avoid her. In the middle of the night, the ache in my back slithered around my body to my stomach, like a worm sensing food. When I woke up, I felt a dampness in between my thighs and quickly flipped off my blanket to see the lower part of my body was covered in blood. I screamed, waking my mother. She screamed twice as loud until the neighbors called the police. An ambulance arrived and put me on a stretcher. When I arrived in the emergency room the doctors confirmed what I already knew. I miscarried.

The chances of being born are one in four hundred trillion and to win that lottery is nothing short of a miracle, one that was denied my child. I could feel the room get emptier as their soul evaporated back into the ether. Once all the viscera had been removed from me, I asked the doctor what sex the child was and he told me it was a girl. From then on, she would haunt me for the rest of my life.

Part Three

Chapter Twenty-Three

Man

My second novel, *Never Too Late*, had my usual moroseness but there was a certain sensitivity to it I was never able to tap into before. It was so good it made me understand where all my previous work was lacking. If I were a publisher, I wouldn't have accepted my earlier shit either but something about this novel hooked everyone I emailed. Suddenly, everyone wanted a piece. I sold it for seventy-five thousand dollars after a bidding war to a publisher in New York city. Fifteen percent of that went to my agent, but I didn't care. This was the first time I ever had any money to spend, save, burn, flaunt or bathe in. Two more books were ordered from me and finally, I had been attuned into authorhood.

From consummate loner, I was now constantly in the company of strangers. The hierarchy of men women fawn over starts at rock star, then A-list movie star. Below the top ten is professional author. Geeky beauties flocked to me after my readings. I'd look out into the audience and see their glossy eyes gazing at me from behind their glasses like I was superhuman. When you become a successful artist, you acquire some kind of superior biology. Your mitochondria shine. Fame triggers evolution.

It became difficult to find time to write, so my agents set me up with a cabin in the middle of backwoods Oregon. Not finding any pain or resentment to take inspiration from, I would try smoking pot all day, writing stream of consciousness poetry until certain lines, ideas, or themes sprung out at me. I did this until the cabin's floor was completely littered with crumpled up, rejected poems.

I voluntarily deprived myself of the internet to make sure my writing wouldn't be politicized. The state of storytelling had been completely poisoned by every hack's aspiration to be an activist. My stories weren't supposed to change laws: they were supposed to enrich lives. One day, a meteor came crashing down from space and landed about three miles from my cabin. Out of curiosity, I traveled to Portland to see the meteor for myself, on the internet. Portland's streets were filled with hipsters, crusties, and nineties nostalgia. I found a cup of coffee in a kitschy little diner that offered free Wi-Fi. I paid a girl at a neighboring booth one hundred dollars to use her phone and log onto my Instagram. I suddenly felt human again, getting to scroll through memes, profiles and ads like the rest of them. It only took about fifteen minutes for my interest in the meteor to pass and I impulsively began looking for Charlotte. I felt like crap for still caring, like I was betraying myself but curiosity took over. It had been five years since the last time I saw her. If it wasn't for her, I wouldn't be the writer I am.

To my surprise, I couldn't find her. She had disappeared without a trace from the internet. I looked everywhere and saw that her television credits came to an abrupt end exactly five years ago. There was no way I could contact her.

I called my agent and told him to cancel my stay at the cabin and I'd take the loss. I decided I needed to return home to Los Angeles. I traveled lightly, just my laptop and I, and when I arrived in L.A., I saw how drastically the city and people had changed. I would actually be recognized among some certain snobby circles. Common people, though, my people, didn't give two shits about me or my book and that's the way I liked it. Literature was once a priority to Americans. It would give their lives meaning, and so writers used to get famous for telling stories. Now, as progress weeds out the various horrors of this world, fame might be the next to go. I can't count how many current famous writers I know on two hands. Think about it. The end of fame, a day when music and movies are just as irrelevant as literature. When no one gives a fuck which actors are in what or who sings for which band. It'll be the dawn of a new age. The fall of Babylon.

There it was. The theme and title of my next book, *The End of*

Fame. The death of the icon. The arts will be filled with people that only create for Eros' sake, not because they want to be remembered. If you wanted to be famous, you'd have to go into politics. I developed these ideas on the road as I embarked on my first full-length book tour across the country. No stone would be left unturned on this tour. I'd visit every trailer park bookstore, ghetto-bird library, and hipster crossover-cafe. City to city, state to state, I kept a mental database of each population's perception of fame. The only way to acquire this data was going out every night and drinking with whichever locals would show me around. I realized that these people would create their own local celebrities. Friends they could vicariously live through. Fame, in that sense, might be a natural expression of hierarchy.

In the two months I spent on the road, I got drunk or high every night. It would be marijuana in the west, cocaine in the north, heroin in the east, and methamphetamine in the south. Luckily for me, as anyone who's ever been close to me has always known, my one superpower is no matter what drugs I take, I never get addicted. I could spend two days snorting cocaine every hour on the hour and not feel any itch to take a bump for a whole five years.

As for the readings themselves, the same kinds of people attended no matter what the city. Hipsters that would laugh at the same things I didn't intend to be funny. Girls with bangs that fell only millimeters above their thick-rimmed glasses. Ninety percent white, sixty percent female, one hundred percent single, one hundred percent depressed and artsy. I read the same passages of the book at every appearance. I read them with the same cadence every time until the words only made sense that one way and I wound up hating my own novel.

This tour pushed the amount of Twitter followers I had to forty thousand. Other writers would tweet about politics, current events, and random musings, always falling into step with the acceptable range of opinions in fear of losing readers. I would tweet my innermost insecurities that had no business on the internet. Each one could've ruined my career or been used against me by some smear campaign. My followers responded with a cult-like devotion to me and acquired an over-protective, homicidal tone when defending me against trolls. One troll though, Danksauce69, was always able to best my followers and me. They were so skilled I couldn't even block them out of pure admiration for their trolling ability. In doing so, they built their own following of about three thousand people. Anything I would say, they would shoot me down. I wouldn't even respond. I'd just take the hits and leave them up for all to see. After one especially destructive comment, I decided to message them directly.

Have you ever read any of my books?

Yeah, you wasted a week of my life and now you're paying for it.

Haven't I already? You've commented on every tweet I've written for the last two months.

No. You still owe me.

What city are you in? I'll buy you a drink and make it up to.

You think I'd ever meet in person with a pervert like you? Yeah right.

The nerve of this guy. He fucked with my head so badly every time I opened Twitter on my phone, I had to check his profile, too. One day, they made a fatal error and retweeted a contest to win two tickets to see a punk band at Saint Vitus' bar in Brooklyn. Danksauce69 was a resident of New York City, where I would be reading at the end of the tour.

Chapter Twenty-Four

Woman

It had been five years since I miscarried and moved back to Brooklyn to live with my mom. Just her, Jinx, and me, in the same apartment I grew up in. Thank God for rent control because the city has turned into a gated community for the rich. Though it's a safer place to live, it certainly doesn't feel like home anymore. Jinx was an old cat now. Oddly, he didn't show any signs of senility. He was still young at heart and didn't have any of the health issues that would have killed a cat his age. Perhaps it was the city that extended his life, because ever since returning to New York, he was happier, stalking the city at night, finding every hidden crevice in between the public guts.

I don't trust anyone but my mother anymore. I've gone five years without sex or a job since my mental and physical breakdown. My only solaces are reading, meditation and a burning desire to not play a role in society. No one needed me anymore. My calendar was completely empty for the next three months. I had no alarm clock or people calling me. My only goal was circled with a red marker on the date of June 6th. That Saturday was a book signing and reading with my favorite author. I bought a ticket four months in advance the moment they went on sale. Two years ago, I began spending my time getting acquainted with this author and all the authors that inspired him. Authors like Henry Miller, Michel Houellebecq, and Neil Gaiman.

My passion for puppetry died with my unborn child so I figured the two must be connected. I am an unworthy vessel of bringing life into this world. Whether it be a puppet I animate or a child I birth. The pain it gives me to admit this is so all-consuming and vicious that if I focused it, it could generate cancer cells in my body. So, I saw this author's reading as a ray of hope. If I could only have a few words with him, I could regain the will to live. That author, was of course, Benjamin Weiss. We're one-one now. He rejected me and I rejected him. I'll be damned if I don't get a tiebreaker.

Ben's love for me felt like obsession or infatuation. Now, after studying lachrymology, I realize obsession is merely love perverted by the pain someone's experienced. The more pain you feel and the more tears you cry, the stranger the way you'll love. Ben Weiss had been hurting for a long time, it made his love weird and because it was a kind of love I couldn't recognize, I just assumed it wasn't good enough for me. Now, after a corpse was purged from my body, the pain I've felt has made my love weird too. So weird only Ben could possibly understand. We were equals now. The world had fucked us both.

Chapter Twenty-Five

Man

Ever since I first came to New York City, I recognized it as the only place on Earth that moves at the same tempo as my mind. We'd go out at night, myself, my agent Shawn, and a gaggle of lit-groupies. It would be a parade of merriment and decadence just on our way to the actual gathering. The subway to the party was its own party.

My first night in Manhattan, I snorted enough cocaine to kill a rhino. It looked like I dropped my keys into a bag of flour. My room at the Hilton was filled with bodies uncomfortably sprawled out on every piece of floor and furniture. I hallucinated sleeping, totally awake until snapping into reality at sunrise, when, upon looking at myself in the mirror, I saw a man I didn't respect. I remembered a time when I knew this wasn't cool.

The drugs, parties, celebration of transgression—it seems this crowd only praises the ugly things in life whether they be serial killers or holocaust jokes or sexual deviancy. Meanwhile, they'd give the real beautiful things like childbirth, marriage or family no notice. They weren't human anymore and I suppose being human means being able to recognize beauty. I was disgusted by us all for us all and thanked God that tomorrow's reading would be the final one.

The audience packed into Barnes and Noble in a single-file line that flooded down the rows of seats. They sat before an empty chair meant for yours truly's ass. Shawn took the microphone to introduce me.

"Hey everybody, thank you for coming out…hope you're as excited for this as I am."

The audience gave me a mighty clap.

"Settle down now, we don't want to scare him away."

...Then a happy chuckle.

"I remember the first time I read Ben's manuscript for *Never Too Late*. I don't think I've ever been more moved by a pile of loose pages. I'm sure, after today, those words will move you too. So, without further ado, please give a warm, New York City welcome to author, Benjamin Weiss."

The audience rose to their feet and applauded me, hollering and whistling as I strode onstage. After the audience sat back down, the first thing I did was scan the room in search for anyone that looked like they could be Danksauce69. I waved at them all with a big smile masking these intentions. Upon looking out at them, I saw her. Sitting in the third row, two chairs from the center aisle. I learned from both our mistakes not to waste opportunities. The last thing I'd do in this moment is hesitate to speak.

"Charlotte, it's good to see you." This side-stepping of the expected chain of events altered the room's tone into something unreal.

There was an awkward silence as every other audience member had no clue what was about to happen.

"It's good to see you too, Ben," she answered, still sitting.

"You read my book?"

"Yes."

"Did you like it?"

"Very much."

I sat down and kept staring right at her. I set my book down beside me so it wouldn't distract me from the reason I was here now.

"Ladies and gentlemen, this is Charlotte...I was once very in love with her."

"I came here hoping to talk to you," she replied.

"You came to an author's reading to talk?" one man cynically blurted out.

We both simultaneously blushed.

"Get that guy the hell out of here," I instructed security, pointing the bastard out.

They grabbed him but not before he took out his phone and started recording video, haranguing me over my now-public clusterfuck romance.

"Bitch ass, Ben Weiss, pussy. Couldn't even get the girl, crying like a bitch. *Danksauce69, ya'll.* Follow me on Twitter."

He was thrown out onto the street as the audience laughed their asses off.

"Do you want to talk after the reading?" I asked Charlotte, cutting through the laughter.

"Please."

"I'll come right up to you."

The reading only lasted twenty minutes because I became so anxious to talk to Charlotte it distracted me into all sorts of stutters and misreadings. Once we were wrapped, I quickly floated over to her and escorted her out so we could leave in the same taxi.

"Where are we going?"

"I'm staying at the Midtown Hilton. We could grab a drink or a smoke there if you'd like."

"Good, I brought my weed."

"So, what have you been up to? Do you live in New York now?"

"I do. I've been pretty much up to nothing."

"Nothing?"

"I had a bad break up in L.A. I had to leave."

"Was it that asshole I poured my drink on at your birthday?"

"Totally. Thank you for that." She smiled at me.

I don't know who inched in closer first but in the back of that taxi, cruising through midtown traffic, we kissed for the very first time. Suddenly, I knew beyond any wealth or success, she was the key to my happiness. We looked forward, pink in the face, our minds swirling with too much epiphany to look directly at each other.

"What a crazy world."

"I know."

I bought her dinner and wine at the Hilton. Without fear, we got right into the life or death questions.

"Do you think there's still a chance for us?" I asked.

"I think there's more than just a chance. Is it what you want?"

"More than anything. You haven't been in my life for years but I'll commit every moment from here on in to you without even a second thought."

"How do you know I'm the one?"

"I've always known. Charlotte, you and I are made for each other."

Her hand was trembling as it reached for her wine and she took a sip.

"I'm not scaring you, am I?"

"No…." she leaned forward and caressed my cheek. "You're not, you sweet and beautiful man."

We kissed and at that moment I silently swore off all foolishness. No more drugs or fucking around. No more self-loathing or fame-whoring. No more posing as a devil when Charlotte needed an angel.

"What do we do from here if we want to fall in love with each other?"

"The wrong way would be going out like a normal couple. To movies, bars, dinners and concerts. We've lost any hope of normalcy with how we've acted toward each other in the past. We have to do something totally different and new."

"I have an idea."

"Shoot."

"Let's go camping," I suggested.

"In nature?" She seemed put off.

"Just you, me, the trees, birds, bugs, and flowers."

She took a big gulp.

"What's wrong?"

"Nothing. Let's do it."

I cancelled my flight back to Los Angeles and the next day Charlotte took me to her apartment in Brooklyn. Brooklyn's poetry was bold enough to be felt in every step. It was absorbed into the concrete and the bums sleeping on sidewalks would inherit the dreams of all the dead poets that came before them. Charlotte's apartment was small but beautiful in its own way. Every detail of the place was a puzzle piece that patched together the gestalt of what her upbringing must've been like. The moment I met her mother, I could tell by the way she looked at me, quickly scanning me from my shoes to my curls, she knew this man standing before her was destined to take care of her daughter.

"Hello, there."

"Are you the Ben I've heard so much about?"

"I hope so."

"Can I hug you?"

"Of course."

She gripped me tightly, with firm squeezes that reaffirmed my belonging in this family. Through osmosis, her lifelong responsibility to protect her daughter had been transferred into me. I could feel my cells reproduce with new purpose.

Charlotte took me into her room while her mother made tea for us. I saw the inner recesses of her mind decorating every inch of her walls. Puppets, cartoons, stuffed animals, and a cat. Charlotte pointed to the cat who squinted at me defensively.

"That's Jinx. If we're going to be a couple, you two have to become friends."

"Hi, Jinx."

I put my hand out to pet him and he hissed at me with his fangs protruding, ready to bite. I snapped my hand back and turned to Charlotte, shamefully shaken. She seemed furious at Jinx.

"What the hell is your problem?" she asked Jinx then turned to me. "Sorry, he's very protective of me."

"It's all right, we just need to warm up to each other."

"Hear that, Jinx? Ben wants to be your friend."

Disinterested, Jinx jumped up on her bed then skittered out the window, leaving us to our boring devices. Now alone, I sat on the bed.

"I like your room. You've got great taste," I told her.

"Funny…you taste great."

She sat on my lap and started kissing me. Pushing my chest down to lay me flat on her bed. Her face enveloped my view of the ceiling and we got lost in each other's lips and tongues.

"Charlotte, tea is ready!" her mother shouted from the kitchen.

Charlotte rose up off my chest and to her feet. I looked at her for a brief moment as the light hit her in this strikingly subtle Vermeer painting way.

"What?" she asked me.

"You're so beautiful. It rips my heart to pieces seeing someone as beautiful as you."

She smiled at me without dwelling on the words too long, stashing them away into a memory bank of reasons she loved me endlessly.

"Come on, kiddo. Your tea's getting cold."

The tea was too hot to drink so I gently blew on it to cool it down before taking tiny sips. Charlotte grabbed my left hand as it rested on the table and began caressing it with her thumb in a circular motion.

"Charlotte tells me you're Jewish," her mother said.

"Yes."

"Mazel tov," she congratulated Charlotte, smiling and batting her eyes.

"Are you religious?" I asked her mother.

"I was raised Catholic but as I grew, I discovered spirituality without the church. To think there's a place people burn forever if they just don't say they're sorry? Are we really supposed to believe child molesters can get into heaven if they apologize? Oh, I forgot, Jews don't believe in hell, do they?"

"I'm not sure. Here, I'll Google it."

"You're as Jewish as we are Catholic."

I looked up 'Jewish hell' on my phone and beside the antisemitic cartoons, I found some pretty interesting insights.

"There's a place called 'Sheol' in the books of Numbers. It's a deep dark pit also known as the land of forgetfulness."

"That's where I hope I go then. I'd forget all about Charlotte's father."

"Mom, stop," Charlotte jeered.

"What about him?" I asked.

"He was a deadbeat musician. Do you play music?"

"Nope."

"Wonderful."

"I just write books."

"I suppose that's better but not by much. Save your money, dear."

All day and night, the thought of finally making love to Charlotte was spinning through my mind. I might've seemed collected but really, I was terribly nervous underneath it all. Once the tea was finished and we were alone again in her room, Charlotte got right back on top of me.

"*Where were we....*"

We began making out again until Jinx returned to her room and jumped onto my face, stabbing it with his claws, breaking us apart.

"Oh shit!" He startled me.

"Jealous much?" Charlotte asked Jinx, batting him away.

Jinx hissed at me again then began pissing on the floor.

"Oh my God...*you really went there?*" Charlotte shouted at the pissing cat.

She ran to her bathroom to get a wet towel and dab the piss out of the carpet. Getting on her knees and cleaning up the mess, she turned to me, rolling her eyes.

"Shit. Sorry, Ben."

"It's all good, babe."

"The smell of cat piss really kills the mood. Maybe you should go."

"Okay. When can I see you next?"

She stood up and grabbed my crotch.

"Go back to your hotel and pack your things to go camping. I'll buy a tent. We'll leave tomorrow."

"Sounds good."

She removed her hand, revealing a bulge pushing up against my jeans. She smiled at me as her eyes floated back up to my face.

"Can you drive?" she asked.

"Yeah."

"Cool, we'll take my mom's Volvo."

Chapter Twenty-Six

Woman

Our Disney princess tent stuck out like a sore thumb in the middle of the heavy forest. I've mentioned this before, I think nature is evil, but in this tent, we were safe from all her demonic forces. Dante's dark woods of error, the place he traversed before entering into hell, could turn out to be a metaphor for this trip. I made sure to bring lots of food, drinks and weed. After we pitched the tent and sat inside making out for a bit, I lit a joint.

"Smoke this."

I took a hit and exhaled into his face then passed him the joint.

"I'm sorry for what this might do to me."

After sucking on the joint three times, exhaling one big cloud of smoke and having his pupils spiral out in a dizzying gesture, his face took on a dopey droop.

"We're a lot alike, don't you think?" he asked.

"In some ways. We're totally different in others."

"Do you think I'm a narcissist?"

"No. I think you're sappy. Do you think you're a narcissist?"

"I worry about it sometimes."

"Why would you think that?"

"I don't know, I wrote this book about you..."

"So, it *was* about me? Ha. I knew it."

Ben laughed. "Let me finish...I wrote this book about you, presuming everything you felt but how was I supposed to know? Really, it was how I wanted you and women in general to feel about me, right? So, doesn't that make me a narcissist?"

"No. Some of the things my character did were kind of weird but I forgive you for that. I see you as desperate, not narcissistic."

"Desperate?"

"You tried and failed to get me so many times you had to write a book to win me over. Lucky for us, it worked. Thank God. Someone had our backs and let it get published."

"You wouldn't have loved me if I wasn't famous?"

"You're not famous."

"If I wasn't successful?"

"Would any woman have done that?"

"I'm not asking about any woman."

"If you came back into my life, in New York…Yeah, I would've fallen in love with you. I wouldn't have cared what you did for a living."

"That makes me feel better."

"It should…you hungry?" I opened up our cooler and reached in to grab the special hero sandwich I made especially for us to share.

"Yeah, eating on weed sounds like a good idea."

I rolled my eyes and laughed through my lips. *Pffft*. I then split the sandwich in two, handing him his half.

"What's in this?" he asked.

"All kinds of nutritious stuff. If anything tastes weird, trust me, it's good for you."

"Okay."

We started eating and I could tell he noticed the secret ingredient I packed into the hero.

"Tastes like old popcorn…and the texture sucks. It's getting stuck in my teeth. What's in it?"

"You really want to know?"

"*Oh my God*…it's shrooms, isn't it?"

"You're smarter than I thought. Now finish your sandwich and don't make a fuss, this is going to be amazing."

"I've always been afraid of psychedelics. Done pretty much everything else."

"I'm the opposite. I guess now you're going to face your fears."

We each finished then kissed with teeth covered in brown bits of dry fungus. The trip set in quickly, dastardly.

"Nothing scares me more than the thought of losing you," he cracked.

"The only way that'll happen is if I die, Ben."

"I won't let you."

"I know."

After a few minutes making out, I accidently bit into his lip too hard and he jerked his face away from mine.

"I'm sorry," I said.

A drop of blood formed on his bottom lip but he didn't seem too upset. He touched the wound with his finger then looked at his finger to examine the blood.

"Does this mean we can't kiss anymore?" he asked, as if it was up to me to make every decision now, which was always the case anyway.

"No."

"Good."

"Do you want me to bleed too?"

"No."

"*Are you sure?*"

"Why would I want you to get hurt?"

"Because I hurt you...I think I want to be hurt too."

"That kind of logic is why we took so long to get together."

"How so?"

"When we met each other in Los Angeles. You wanted revenge...for me rejecting you. Some mistakes should go unpunished."

Such a spiteful statement was enough to snowball into a relationship's end but I decided to take his advice. I wasn't going to not punish him for the rest of his life by stranding him in the forest alone.

"Maybe you are a narcissist if you really think that. I didn't want you because you couldn't give me what I needed or wanted at that moment of my life."

"What I have to give you now is the exact same thing as what I had to give you then."

"You're right but five years ago, I couldn't see that."

"Why not?"

"I was immature. I grew up."

He was silent after that, for whatever reason it was a point he couldn't dispute.

"Do you want to go for a walk?" he asked.

"Like outside?"

"Yeah."

"Sure, but you have to protect me against the demons."

He unzipped the tent open, letting in all the world's evil in a breath. We crawled out onto the soil and holding hands, began traversing through Dante's dark woods. It was a rather timid patch of nature. The calming songs of birds and the buzzing of insects settled all my reservations. Upon seeing the first mushroom sprouting out of a dead tree, the psilocybin began its ascent up our spines and into our brains.

"Nature is evil. Left to its own devices, it consumes without limit. Civilization was man's last line of defense against this evil. It was a creation of goodness. A shield and sword. When man dies, good will die with him, returning Earth to its natural state of darkness, evil, torment, and corruption."

"Maybe you're right, but you can't deny the benevolence of this place, right now. Walking among the plants and animals as if there were no boundaries between us."

"I feel at one with chaos. Like a living manifestation of the possibility that anything can happen."

"Anything?"

He kissed me but I was in too deep of a haze to respond to romance. Romance seemed far removed from this primitive state of mind. Did the apes know true love? Did Adam and Eve? What did the custom of giving a rose mean in the garden of Eden? Surrounded by splendor, without competition, romance is arbitrary. Pulling away, he looked at me rather curious.

"Do you feel it?"

"Sorry. Yeah, I'm high as fuck."

"What's it feel like to you?"

"Euphoric but also introspective. I can see our puppet strings from heaven, controlling our every move. What about you?"

He compulsively burst into tears before he could answer. Stoic one moment and shattered the next, I feared he was having a bad trip. Through my eyes, the shrooms pronounced the highlights all around us, godly rays emanating onto coiling forest. Through his eyes, only shadows, reaching up from below, grabbing at our insecurities and pulling them out our chests to obstruct all connection. I ran my hand through his hair, trying to restore his sanity.

"It's okay, baby. I'm here."

"Never leave me," he squeaked, curling up into a ball, like a roly-poly preparing for a child's death pinch.

"I won't," I assured him.

We held each other, rocking back and forth in the same place for what must've been thirty minutes, the blink of a dreaming God's eye. Once he collected himself enough to stand, we kept venturing through the forest until reaching a cliff that gave us the perfect view of the sunset. As the sun dipped into the horizon and cut open the sky, all those delicious hues of color it hid under its skin bled out. We felt a closeness the end of time would have trouble breaking.

"Do you think we act like children? The way we love each other?"

"If we do, it's a good thing."

"Most people, they don't fall in love so easily, do they? It's kind of what kids do, right?"

"It's what people that haven't been loved do. It's easy to love someone more than your own life when your life has been shit, and that's us, until now. Our lives are beautiful."

Before total darkness descended upon us, we returned to the tent, the only consecrated circle of protection in this realm of debasement, slaughter, and sodomy of the spirit. The come-down hit us softly, our scar-tissue brains sore like an acidized muscle but with that soreness, a discomforting relief. Each of us adopted a piece of the abstract. Our love was now less human but more whole. When it was time to sleep, we did everything but. Ben laid down for me to gently unbutton his shirt and jeans. I kissed the bare chest that would come to be my rock and pillow. Once he pulled off his boxers, my mouth began kissing his cock. The mushrooms had nothing on the sex. Our reserve bursts of serotonin gushed out like water from a broken faucet. The whole spectrum of colors was made visible behind my eyes. After a blowjob meant for a king, he sat up and laid back down on his stomach so his mouth met my pussy. He began eating me out with innate knowledge of every fold. Pleasure shot up and down my nervous system making quick work of my body into a porcelain paste.

"Oh my God, I love you so much," I yelped.

I came twice under his tongue's duress until finally, I felt it was time to make love. I flipped him onto his back and sat on top of him, fitting his cock into me. I was his cock's puppet. Words cannot describe this moment because language is a prison and for the first time, we were free.

"Your cock is HUGE."

"Fuck me, baby. Fuck the shit out of me."

I was on top for ten minutes until he took charge and flipped me over into the missionary position. Spreading my legs then propping them up onto his shoulders, I could feel his body trembling and the ribbing of his cock constricting before climax.

"I'm going to cum. I'm going to cum."

"Cum inside me. Cum inside me, please."

He came inside me in a life-defining moment for us both. I had been fucked by every Ben Weiss that ever wanted me. The Ben I went to college with and was too timid to ask me out. The Ben that was broke and too insecure to have me. The Ben that was a rich and successful writer— all came inside me at once.

Once he pulled out and laid by my side, we held each other tightly and kissed.

"I fucking love you," he told me unabashedly.

"I fucking love you too."

Our love had done it. It survived the forest, shrooms, and all the past resentment we held for each other. We were one and meant to be. The future would hold many more hurdles but we'd meet them head-on, hand-in-hand, together, without fear.

Chapter Twenty-Seven

Man

We drove back into the city with new life running through our interlocked hands. I brought her home and she asked me to come in to eat something. So, Charlotte and her mother began making dinner in the kitchen.

"I'm exhausted. You mind if I take a nap?"

"Go for it, dinner will be ready in an hour."

"Thanks babe, love you."

"Love you too," she said and glanced at her mother who smiled back to her.

I droned over to her room and made my way to her bed where Jinx was resting. Forgetting he hated my guts, I sat down next to him and laid backward to relax. Jinx got up and loomed over me, sneering.

"What do you think you're doing?"

The psilocybin must've metabolized in my spine and after lying down and cracking my back, it must have reactivated the high. That's the only possible explanation for a talking cat. That or I'm dying right now and my brain is defensively releasing chemicals to make me hallucinate to distract me from my impending end.

"Hey, fuck face...I'm talking to you."

"How?"

"How am I talking? Through my mouth, retard."

"But...you're a cat."

"Correction. I look like a cat. I am in fact, much more."

"Do you talk to Charlotte too?"

"No way. I have nothing I need to say to her…but you, I got plenty of say to you, fuck-face. Starting with the question…*what the fuck do you think you're doing?*"

"Trying to rest."

"On my fucking bed?"

"It's Charlotte's bed."

"It's our bed, and you got some fucking nerve thinking you can park your ass on it. Especially while I sleep."

"I thought you were a cat. What do you expect?"

"Well, now that you know…what are you waiting for, get the fuck up."

I sighed and stood up off the bed.

"If you break up with her, I swear to fucking God I will scratch out your fucking eyes while you're sleeping and shit in their sockets."

"I'm not going to break up with her. I love her."

"In that case, we'll be seeing quite a bit of each other. If you want me not to make this relationship a living hell for you then you'll have to do as I say. My first order is that tonight you will refuse to eat any food at dinner."

"They'll be so angry."

"Scratch out your eyes, shit in their sockets…*remember?*"

"Fine. I won't eat."

"Good boy, and if you tattle on me…."

"Claw out my eyes, shit in their sockets…*yeah, yeah.*"

"No. I'd be shitting in your mouth in that case."

"Don't worry, kitty, your secret's safe with me."

"You think you're real funny, don't you? Well, you're not gonna have much to laugh about because you're my bitch now and you will do exactly as I say."

"Whatever. I'll see you around, Jinx. Try not to get too jealous."

He hissed at me as I left the room, rolling my eyes.

I stepped into the dining room where plates were already set for three and began holding my stomach, groaning to pretend I had fallen ill. Charlotte stepped into the room carrying a steaming hot hunk of beef to place at the table's center.

"Here, doesn't it smell delicious?"

She lifted the beef to my nose and I met its delicious aroma with feigned disgust.

"Babe, I think I caught the stomach flu because my insides feel all tied up in knots. I'm worried anything I put down is gonna come right back up."

"We just prepared a whole dinner for you."

"It hit me in your room as soon as I lied down. It smells amazing though, I wish I could eat it."

Charlotte's mother came in holding two loaded plates, one with salad and the other with pasta. She set the food down and turned toward us.

"Sit down kids, let's eat."

When I hesitated, her eyes peered at me.

"What's wrong?" She looked at me then parked her eyes on Charlotte, my spokesperson.

"He's not hungry."

Her eyes burned orange with entropic fury, "What do you mean you're not hungry?" she wanted to hear the pathetic excuse come out of my mouth.

"It's not that I'm not hungry, I'm sick."

"Sick? How are you sick?"

"We just came back from camping. Who knows what kind of bacteria or insect copulated in me?"

"This is why I say you always need to bring anti-bacterial everywhere you go," Charlotte's mother lectured.

"How about I sit with you while you eat and take home some leftovers? Maybe I'll feel better tomorrow."

Charlotte and her mother glanced at each other, defeated.

"I suppose that's our only choice," her mother sighed.

Charlotte rolled her eyes then sat down, "Dig in, Mom."

The women sat down and started filling their faces. I heard a quiet creaking and turned my head back to Charlotte's room where Jinx cracked open the door to watch. I nodded at the bastard and he winked at me with human malice. Sitting down with my new family, I watched as they quietly and with disdain for me, enjoyed the delicious-smelling meal.

"So, what are you going to do? Move to New York?" Charlotte's mother broke the silence.

"I think so," I answered quickly.

"It's expensive around here. You'll be paying a house's mortgage for a shithole studio."

"As long as I get to be close to Charlotte, I don't mind."

Charlotte's mother smiled.

"You're all right, you know that, Ben."

"Thanks."

"Hopefully you two are practicing safe sex."

"Mom!" Charlotte shouted.

My eyes darted to Charlotte's the same moment as hers darted to mine.

"Well? Are you?"

"Of course…we're not stupid," Charlotte told her mother.

I had been given three Tupperware boxes of food to take home after dinner. Charlotte and I went onto the fire escape for some privacy. Taking in the inspiration, mood, street music, and a cigarette, I tried to clear the air.

"Should I have not cum in you?"

"We don't have regrets in this relationship. So, the question is irrelevant."

"What if you get pregnant?"

She came in close and rose on her tip-toes to kiss me.

"Then we start a family. We become bound to each other for the rest of our lives through our child. Nothing will ever break that bond."

"Do you think you're ready to be a mom?"

"Yes. For so long everything went wrong in my life but this feels so right, even if we struggle it would be the most perfect life I could have ever lived."

"Okay…I think I'm ready, too…I just don't want to move too fast for you."

"We've been on each other's minds for over a decade, Ben. We've been taking it slow." She smiled.

When I returned to Los Angeles, the first thing I did was buy

Charlotte a ring. If she wanted to be the mother of my child, I wanted her to be my wife. After selling everything I owned in Los Angeles and spending two weeks apart from my baby, I flew back to New York on a Friday with my whole life crammed into a single suitcase. I made special arrangements so when she first saw me treading toward baggage claim, past the gate, my grand plan would begin.

A swarm of puppeteers and people in fuzzy monster body suits followed me out of the terminal toward my awestruck lover. Her jaw dropped and her eyes turned wet. Everyone, inanimate and living, began singing "I Can't Help Falling in Love With You." Her mother stood behind her, shaking her head in joyous disbelief. Our combined years of peril had not been in vain: the struggle had finally proven to have been well worth it as I dropped down to one knee.

"Charlotte, I love you more than my own life. I refuse to live without you. You mean everything to me. I want to spend the rest of my life with you. I need you like my lungs need air to breathe. Charlotte Samantha Green, will you marry me?"

"Yes."

A new and shining sun rose upon our love. Every pair of eyes shed a tear and every pair of hands erupted into applause. I put the ring on her finger and before I could jump up to kiss her, she pounced, toppling us backward onto the floor. Holding each other as we strode outside through the airport's sliding doors, Charlotte's mother kissed me on the head three times, sharing with me a ceaseless gratitude to God.

I picked Charlotte up and carried her in my arms through her bedroom door. When I set her on the bed and started kissing her, she gently pushed me away.

"I'm on my period."

"Shit."

"I know."

"*Soooo*...is sex out of the question?"

She didn't need words to answer, she just slid back and sat up. Jinx purred in the rhythm of an uproarious laugh.

"I wanted to get pregnant."

"We only tried once."

"I know…but I'm still scared."

"Scared of what?"

She started sobbing uncontrollably. I held her tightly, kissing her head and running my fingers through her hair.

"Don't worry, sweetheart. We're going to have a family."

"My body rejects life. I was pregnant once but my body killed the baby. I was too weak. I'm not strong enough to have your child. I don't know why I said yes to your proposal. How could I ever do that to you and get in your way of being a father."

She was hysterical, a pure ball of doubt and pain, a living wound, bleeding all her fears out in front of me.

"I would love you no matter if you could have children or not…that said, you're much stronger than you realize, Charlotte. You're still that cocky, cool girl from college. When these dark voices try to put you down, I'll be there to help you fight them off. I won't let you go down without a fight."

"I can't have sex tonight, Ben. I just need to cry and have you hold me."

"Then I will hold you the whole night through."

My arm fell asleep within an hour but that didn't stop me from wrapping it around her back for half the night. Luckily for me, at three thirty-two a.m., she got up and walked over to the bathroom to piss, freeing me. With no light in the room but the outline of the bathroom door, Jinx hopped up onto my stomach, staring at me with amber eyes.

"It's a shame really, what you're going through."

"What exactly are you referring to?"

"You're seeing Charlotte for who she is. A nice person but a very, very damaged, crazy one."

"Wow…that's what you think of the girl that rescued you off the street?"

"I could've done without. You don't know her like I do, pal. She is a fucking loon."

"I won't let you talk that way about the girl I'm going to marry."

"You won't let me? Have you forgotten our last conversation? Perhaps a small display of my power will refresh your memory."

Right then and there, he casually shit on my stomach.

"Ew, gross. What the fuck is your problem?"

I wiped the poo off but some of its slime stayed on me and began burning my skin.

"What the fuck, my skin feels like it's on fire."

"Lie back down if you want to live."

I did as he said, in too much agony to distrust the sly feline. He peed on my burn, extinguishing the pain and as I sighed with relief, Charlotte flushed the toilet, stepping out of the bathroom.

"What the hell are you shouting for?"

"Sorry, Jinx just peed on me."

"You're kidding…?"

"I wish I was."

She scooped him up by the tail and opened the window to set him outside. She then closed the window, locking him out.

"You're on timeout, motherfucker. Don't come back until you think about what you've done."

Jinx happily jumped down the fire escape.

"He's been acting up ever since we started dating."

"You wouldn't ever think of getting rid of him, would you?"

"No way. We're just going to have to tough it out."

"That's fine. How much trouble can a cat really be anyway?"

Chapter Twenty-Eight

Woman

I never told this to Ben but after I miscarried, the reason I moved back to New York wasn't just because I needed my mommy. I left because I tried to take my own life by overdosing on Xanax. I needed to get rid of the guilt and that didn't seem possible if I was still thinking. I felt just as responsible for my miscarriage as a murderer does for taking the life of their victim. My unconscious body was discovered by my mother and after getting my stomach pumped, I didn't wake up until days later in a hospital.

It was a miracle I only suffered minor brain damage but it only seemed to affect my emotions, not my cognizance. The coma felt like napping on a canoe that was floating on a sea of non-existence. Perennial Viking funeral. I touch the same feeling every time I meditate. It's a state more basic and elementary than thinking, it is raw being. Death is only one conceptual rung beneath a coma, so for me, death doesn't take much of a leap to imagine. What I'm trying to say is I'm not afraid of death. What I am afraid of is not living up to my potential of being a mother. Loving Ben has reaffirmed my clairvoyance to me. Having a son and experiencing the world's end are the only visions that have yet to materialize. Had I not miscarried, it would have negated my clairvoyance.

~ * ~

Ben got an apartment a few blocks away with enough room that we could lie down next to each other. We were having sex every night and not wasting a drop of his seed. Still though, no matter how much I drained him,

I wasn't getting pregnant. We tried everything, even seeing a doctor and getting tested for sterility. The results told us to just keep trying because both of our bodies were made to procreate. Taking advice from the internet, Ben changed his diet, routine, and wardrobe to stimulate his virility, producing stronger, smarter, more agile sperm. Every month, my period would rear its ugly head and crush my hopes until our nightly sex was replaced with my nightly crying. I was so emotionally fragile I couldn't walk five minutes through my neighborhood without breaking down. I'd cry seeing other children or things I'd like to buy my child. Ben did his part, being a good man, being patient with me, buying me flowers. He realized bringing me out of this rut would be difficult and doing so would require matching my pain with love. I didn't get over it but eventually, I stopped crying, replacing that routine with smoking enough weed every day to drive anyone crazy.

~ * ~

Molly and Esa were dying to meet Ben. I hadn't spoken to them since Ben moved to New York. Now that they knew the man I had been talking about since college was finally my fiancé, the girls had to meet him and approve. The four of us met on the subway train to brunch. The three of us girls sat side by side on the busy train car while Ben stood by our side, looming over us. I could tell Molly thought he was handsome. There was a certain admiration in her eyes. Esa on the other hand, was masterfully hiding a scowl.

"How much has Charlotte told you about us?"

"Well, I know about your Moose tattoo and therapy office, doctor."

Molly and I started laughing hysterically while Esa raised an eyebrow, shaking her head too subtly to call out. Ben made us go to a deli, pitching this place as one of the oldest restaurants in New York. Us girls ordered the most basic American food on the menu while Ben got chopped liver and herring shmeared on a bagel.

"Is Charlotte going to convert for you?" Esa asked.

"To what? Weissism?" I asked.

"She's already a believer," Molly joked.

Ben smirked and answered, "It hasn't really come up…I'm happier than I've ever been, I'm not going to ask her to change a damn thing."

After a few more bites of food, Esa kept poking at Ben, "I read your book."

"What did you think?"

"Not a fan."

"Why not?"

"You portray women as powerless fools that only acquire strength from man. If that's your idea of femininity, I don't know how you got published."

I cringed at how awkward I felt but Ben just kept chomping away at his bagel, bits of chopped liver on his lips, like nothing could phase him.

"Do you need me, Charlotte?" he asked me.

"Yes," I answered.

Ben shrugged at Esa, "I need her too. There ya go. See, the men in my stories aren't portrayed so great either. They're often weak, dependent, impotent, insecure, and shallow. So, I guess you could say I'm not too hot on people in general, including myself."

Esa rolled her eyes then turned from Ben to me. "As long as you're happy."

"Are you happy, Esa?" I asked her.

"Not for you."

The conversation had the wind knocked out of it until Esa got up and threw her share of the bill on the table.

"Sorry to be a buzzkill, love you, Charlotte, Molly."

Esa gave Ben the cold shoulder then walked out of the deli, leaving us.

"Joke's on her, I was going to get the bill," Ben laughed.

"Don't mind her. The truth is she's always been in love with Charlotte," Molly said, shaking her head.

"You know she tried to make out with me once," I stated.

"*What? No… When?*" Molly's eye grew wide.

"When you visited me in L.A. She tried to make a pass at me in a bar bathroom then blamed it on being drunk."

"*Oh my God… Why are you only telling me this now?*"

"I didn't want anything to come between our friendship."

"Babe, her and I only see each other when you're involved. All my friends are hipsters like Ben."

"I am not a hipster."

She stared at him in a patronizing way. "You are, you just can't grow a beard."

Once the food was eaten and paid for, Molly and I went into the restroom to make a final verdict inside two separate stalls.

"So, what do you think of him?"

"He's cool. Seems like he's got money, what more could you ask for?"

"Plenty, babe."

"Like what?"

"We've been trying to have a baby for months but nothing is working."

"He looks like he's shooting blanks."

"The doctor said he was fine."

"Well, that's a shitty situation to be in. You're at that point of your life if it doesn't happen now, then it ain't ever gonna happen."

"Don't you feel scared, for yourself?"

"It's 2025. It's better for the environment not to have kids."

Like clockwork, we flushed and finished our business. That night in Ben's apartment, the potential for love-making was in the air. I felt like rewarding him for how he acted in front of my friends.

"Did you like Molly and Esa?"

"Yeah. Both of them."

"What Esa said didn't bother you?"

"Not really. I like strong personalities. If I'm their target every once in a while, it's a small price to pay for society to have some balls."

"I'm glad you liked them," I said and looked at him suggestively.

"Anyone that's a friend of my girl must be brilliant."

We shared an Eskimo kiss until our cuteness very slyly transformed into passion and our noses disconnected to let our lips meet. I ran my hand down his chest, telling him I wanted more on this new moon night. Once he got the message, I was on my back with a giant Jew pressed against me.

After a few thrusts, I almost broke out into tears. The sex wasn't what it used to be, they felt like the pumps of a defeated man, trying to pop my bubble of low expectations with his cock. His body knew I was upset with it and succumbed to his mind's insecurity. He couldn't even cum this time. He heaved off of me and was so oblivious he even fucking apologized.

"Sorry, I don't know what happened."

"Neither do I," I said, referring to everything ever between us.

He was too spent to argue so we went to sleep incomplete. It felt wrong on so many levels but again, I thought I was to blame. The next morning, after he left the apartment to either get us breakfast perhaps cheating on me on the way, I masturbated my pain away, went into his bathroom, and dove under the sink to explore my options for suicide. I had two. Bleach or razor. I chose the razor and drew a bath. The water would turn a precious pink when marrying my blood. I got into the bath without hesitating, slicing upwards, deeply and with precision, the way you cut through ham. Severely severing the real, sir. I lay back and watched the grid of tiles on the wall blur into one white light.

Ben found me minutes from death, his screams a bit muffled by my shock. He tied towels around my wrist to stop the bleeding and called the police. He kept slapping my cheeks to make sure at all costs I wouldn't drift away from him. In mere moments, an ambulance arrived and took me to the hospital. What was funny was my mother arrived before me, tears in her eyes and shame written all over her face. She felt sorry for Ben.

Chapter Twenty-Nine

Man

There was no going back now. Immediately, everyone that loved Charlotte began hating me, not based on the substance of my character but on their love and desire to protect their girl. The only person that felt sympathy for me was Charlotte's mother, who was sure I was no longer the right man for her daughter. I was a good man that caused her to harm herself. Perhaps a therapist would be a good man for Charlotte, or a straitjacket. I couldn't stop shaking or crying in the emergency room. The staff was tending to me like I was the one that raced here in an ambulance. Charlotte's mother couldn't stop pacing the hallways. We both knew she would survive but our future together would die after this.

"She did this once before. Did she ever tell you that?"

"No."

"She tried to overdose after her miscarriage."

"Fuck...I didn't know."

"You didn't say anything to upset her?"

"For the last time, no."

"This was all because she couldn't get pregnant."

"That's what I think."

"She needs professional help," Charlotte's mother said, bursting into tears. "I can't take care of her anymore," she commiserated.

"You're not putting her in a mental institution. I won't let you. She's my fiancée."

"You can't do anything for her now, Ben. You're hurting her."

As a writer, the only tools I was equipped with to fix this situation were my words. I could eloquently tell her how much she mattered to me and everyone. More than that, I could write and tame our monstrous feelings into prose. I swore on that day I would use the pen to affirm life and not death. The hospital's chaplain came around asking if we wanted to pray together and though I declined, I asked to borrow his Bible to read Proverbs 18:21.

"The tongue has the power of life and death, and those who love it will eat its fruit."

Both God and my father were absent from my life at this time. It's been months since we've spoken. So, after consulting the good book, I gave my old man a ring.

"Yes?"

"Dad, I need your help."

"What happened?"

"Charlotte tried to take her own life."

"Dear God. Is she all right?"

"She'll live. We're at the hospital."

"Are you with her right now?"

"No. I'm in the E.R. hallway crying my fucking eyes out. I don't think we're getting married anymore." I began sobbing uncontrollably.

"Calm down. Breathe…" my father waited for me to calm then continued. "How did she do it?"

"She found a razor under my sink." The tears started flowing. "I was out getting us breakfast."

"This isn't your fault, Ben."

"What do I do? Her mother wants to put her in a nut house."

"She goes in there and she's lost forever. They'll put her on enough pills to zombify her till the day she dies. Then your fiancé will really be gone."

"I'm not going to let that happen. I don't give a fuck."

"Do you need me to come to you?"

"No."

"I can talk to her mother. I can help her understand."

"No. That's okay, Dad."

"Your father knows what he's talking about, Ben. I can fix this."

I was sobbing so hard, I could barely get a word out but my father heard enough anyway.

"This is what happens, Ben. This is what your mother was trying to warn you about. These people have different values than you. You were raised to respect the sanctity of life. You were raised to take care of the ones you love from the cradle to the grave no matter what fucking happens. You shoulda loved a Jew, goddamn it."

"I'm sorry. I'm so fucking sorry."

"Don't be. It's not your fucking fault." I hung up, unable to take another second of him.

Charlotte's mother refused to let me see her daughter. She assured me I could visit in a couple days once she recovered.

Walking around the city in a haze, the pain inside me felt something like my skin being torn string by string. I couldn't go home, to the scene of the suicide attempt. Instead, I decided I would go to her apartment and confront the mother fucker I felt was partially responsible for this. I reached the foot of her apartment building and stood below the fire escape's raised ladder. I pushed over a dumpster to climb on top of and reach the ladder's first rung. From there, I climbed the ladder then the stairs up to her bedroom window on the other side of which, Jinx was already waiting for me, smiling.

"What's wrong?" he asked.

My faced flushed furious as I started looking for something to break through the window. After finding nothing, I took off my shirt, wrapped it around my fist, and punched through the glass. Jinx jumped backward as my hand went through the window. I opened it from the inside and stepped into the bedroom.

"Don't be mad at me, I tried to warn you," Jinx explained.

"Do you know why she did this?"

"Probably because you couldn't knock her up, pencil dick."

"So, it *is* my fault?"

"Yeah, but so what? It ain't easy getting a girl pregnant, couples struggle with that all the fucking time, doesn't mean you have to slit your wrists."

The fist I clenched in preparation of punching this cat went limp and fell by my side. My knees started to shake until buckling and I fell upon them to cry in the room in which my Charlotte would sleep.

"What do I do? Her mother wants to put her in an asylum."

"The hell she will, who's going to take care of me then?"

"This isn't about you, Jinx."

"Yes, it is, *dumbass*. I'm the only one who can fix this."

"You can?"

"For a price."

"Explain exactly what you mean as clearly as you can."

"I can cast a spell on you that will guarantee the next time you sleep with Charlotte, she will be impregnated with child. The spell will also make sure the child is born healthy. If Charlotte is pregnant there's no way her mother will keep her in an asylum."

"Then cast the spell. I'll do anything."

"I doubt you'll be so eager when I tell you what you have to pay."

"You want my life? I'll give you my life."

"Not your life but your soul. You will give me your eternal soul so I may trade it to the devil."

"The devil? As in hell? Like fire and brimstone?"

"Your expectations of hell are inaccurate. You will have to see for yourself."

"If I have to die and go to hell for eternity just so my wife can live a happy, normal life then I will do it."

"This means all your dreams of being a writer will be lost."

"How would I be able to live knowing she's in agony and there's nothing I can do to help her?"

"So, do you agree to the terms of this deal? I cast a spell that will guarantee to get her pregnant and you give me your soul to trade to the devil."

I could feel a gentle breeze wisp through the broken window. I took in a deep breath and with full faith, answered Jinx.

"Yes."

Jinx jumped on top of me and licked my nose. He then sat back down in front of me.

"Now, all you have to do is fuck her."

"That's it? You licked me, now my dick is magic?"

"What did you expect me to do? Pull a wand out of my ass?"

"I guess not... How am I supposed to have sex with her if she's in the hospital?"

"Figure it out. You have twenty-four hours."

"What if I can't find a way?"

"Your soul will still be mine. Sorry. I guess you really do love her though. I don't think anyone can question that now."

"What happens after I succeed?"

"I'll find you."

"Okay."

I stood up and made my way out the window. After I stuck one leg out, Jinx stopped me for a second.

"I know we haven't always had the most pleasant relationship, but I like you, Ben."

I blankly stared at him with nothing to say.

"I will be with you on this journey. You won't go through hell alone."

The sun set on my path to the hospital. I waited outside the hospital until after midnight, suspicious of everyone like they were a potential threat. Once I felt the time was right, I filled myself with enough inertia to storm the gates. I walked through the emergency room's sliding doors as if I had every right to go wherever I pleased. I nodded at the receptionist and she buzzed me in through the locked door to the hallway. I treaded quickly and lightly, as if with Jinx's feet. Employees passed by me at either side, all in too much of a hurry to question my motives. When I arrived at Charlotte's room, I peeked in to see her mother sitting by her side, stoic and immovable. I took a deep breath and stepped into the forbidden room.

"Motherfucker. I told you to stay away," her mother growled.

Charlotte was Sleeping Beauty, drained of all life but that which was being shot into her veins through a system of tubes.

"I had to see her, Victoria. She is the love of my life."

"You almost killed her."

"I will not stand for you saying that. I am her rock and she is mine. You don't have the power to tear us apart."

"I won't have you disturbing her peace. I'm calling security."

"Mom…please," spoke Charlotte, still half asleep.

Charlotte stirred awake. She knew I was in the room somewhere deep in her unconscious.

"Sweetie, you're not in your right mind. He shouldn't be here."

"I need him now."

"Charlotte…sweetheart." My heart was tearing to pieces as the words left my lips.

"Mom…you need to leave me and Ben alone for ten minutes."

Charlotte's mother kept her anguish under wraps.

"If anything happens, I'll be right outside."

She glared at me on her way out and I floated over to my lover's side.

"Sit with me, Ben."

She scooched over on her hospital bed giving me room to sit. With my ass touching hers, I felt how cold she was. I took her hand in mine and gripped it tightly.

"I should have come sooner."

"I wish you did."

"I'm sorry, Charlotte. I love you so much."

"No, Ben. I'm sorry, I made such a mistake."

"You need to know how much you mean to me and so many other people."

"I didn't do this because I didn't think I mattered."

"You did it because we couldn't have a baby."

Her sleepy, dying eyes began to fill with tears. She nodded at me somberly.

"What if I told you that I found a way to give you a child?"

"How?"

"Magic."

She smiled at me. I expected her to cynically reject the idea but surprisingly, she took it seriously.

"*Go on.*"

"A wizard put a spell on me. If we have sex, you will get pregnant and the child will be born healthy."

"What are you waiting for, stud? *I believe in magic.*"

"Are you strong enough to make love?"

"I was strong enough to kick my mother the fuck out of here. Don't worry about me, you just get your head in the game, I know I'm not exactly sexy right now, hospitals in general aren't a good place to...."

"I'm already hard, babe."

While I was in Charlotte's hospital room, summoning up my libido against its will, Jinx made his way to the E.R., past all the guards and employees, until finding Charlotte's mother waiting outside our closed door. Jinx silently crept right up to her and without her noticing, licked her ankle. Just like that, she collapsed into a peaceful sleep.

Meanwhile, inside our emergency room abode, Charlotte sucked me as hard as I was going to get and so I laid on top of her, inserting myself. Thrusting in and out of her, I took my mind into a place devoid of all the limpening distractions around me. I honed in on the enveloping feeling of her, just the ecstasy of sex and nothing more. It wasn't long until I shot into her the will to live in the form of our promised child. I removed my penis from her, got up, then kissed her on the head.

"I will love you forever. Long after I am dead. Our child will never let you down and you mustn't ever let him down."

"It's going to be a boy?"

"Yes...I have to go now."

"Where?"

"I'm not sure."

"Please don't. Stay with me just a little bit longer."

"I can't."

Suddenly, the door opened and in walked Jinx.

"Jinxy? What are you doing here?" Charlotte asked.

Jinx then jumped up onto her bed.

"Good luck, Charlotte...and thanks for everything," Jinx told her.

"*What the fuck...*You can...."

Jinx licked her hand and she fell right to sleep just like her mother.

"Don't worry, she's only sleeping," Jinx assured me.

"What now?"

"Follow me."

Jinx led me out of the hospital and into the city. Skittering down the stairs into the subway, I could sense this journey would only take us in one direction and that was down. The subway station was completely empty. Jinx jumped down onto the tracks, waiting for me to follow. I hesitated for a moment.

"Come on, don't be scared. It's not like you got a life to lose any more anyway," Jinx implored.

I sighed and followed him onto the tracks and into the darkness of the tunnel. After a few minutes trekking in this darkness, Jinx came upon a hole in the ground and jumped down. I couldn't see where the hole led but it didn't matter. I jumped down and free fell into the black. I landed on my ass atop a giant black pillow set over a stone walkway in another tunnel. This tunnel appeared ancient. It was lit by torches on either side. Jinx sat beside me, waiting for me to stand and as I did, I looked ahead to see three angels guarding a gate.

"Who goes there?" the angel on the left asked with a bellowing voice.

The angel standing to the left had black wings and golden eyes. The angel in the middle had white wings and white eyes. The angel to the right had golden wings and black eyes.

"I am Octavius, shadow of the saintly owl, feline ambassador to Earth," Jinx introduced himself to the angels.

"Octavius?" I asked laughing as Jinx rolled his eyes.

"State your business," demanded the angel in the middle.

"This man gave me his soul in exchange for a wish. I granted him his wish and am escorting him to hell to trade his soul to Lucifer."

The angels' eyes all panned over at me.

"Benjamin Weiss, I am the angel of fear," said the angel with black wings and golden eyes.

"How do you know my name?" I asked.

"By looking into your eyes. By looking into mine, can you guess my name, Ben?" the angel to left asked.

It took me a moment. Its eyes seemed defeated and broken and its wings sunk low on its shoulders as if clipped by the weight of its shame.

"Shame," I guessed.

"I suppose it's written all over my face. There's nothing I can do about it," Shame said and hung its head.

"And you?" I asked the angel in the middle.

"Chastity," it said in a high, virginal voice.

"Before we let you pass, we must judge you, Ben."

"Why?" Jinx asked.

"Because if Ben is worthy, we will buy his soul off you and ensure it doesn't go to hell."

"I'm open to the idea if the price is right."

"The three of us will now look into Ben's eyes to see the totality of his life's good deeds and sins. His accomplishments and his failures. His friends and enemies. After assigning him a value, we will tell you our verdict."

I felt like I was under a hot spotlight, sweating as the three angels stared holes into my head.

"Well, I know what I'd like to do," Fear spoke.

"Same," said Chastity.

"I'm so sorry, Ben. I did it again, messed up another person's eternity," Shame said.

"What's the verdict?"

"We pass," said Fear.

"Hell can have you, Ben," Chastity spoke.

Chastity was rather rude, I thought.

"Didn't I do well on Earth? My life wasn't wasted," I defended myself.

"Sure it was. If you didn't trade your soul and just died naturally, you would've still gone to hell."

"Really?"

"Yeah. You pretty much didn't care about anyone but yourself for the majority of your life."

"Until Charlotte."

"How long did it take you to show it? How long were you two actually together? Less than a year?"

"You had no fear of God in your life. Spitting on his law and ruining your health, you were completely devoid of values."

"Not true. What about the parable of the talents? I knew I was a talented writer and I risked my life to become a professional. I didn't waste what God gave me."

"*Awww*, you were a writer?" Chastity asked, patronizingly. "Well, that changes everything. Hear that guys? He made art, so *clearly* he deserves to go to heaven…"

"Okay, I get it…" I rolled my eyes.

"Here's an idea for your next book title. How about, *My Flesh Rots and My Soul Burns for Eternity in This Godless Hell That I Deserve*?"

"Hell is staying here with you three. Let's go, Jinx," I said.

The three angels cracked up like a gaggle of devils. Callously, they opened the gate to hell and stepped aside to let us pass through. The inhumanity of the angels gave me a certain serenity, knowing even in heaven there would've been no sympathy or mercy for me. Jinx and I traveled further down the tunnel to a pair of golden doors that sat beside a button. Jinx hopped up to press the button and the golden doors slid open. It was an elevator. We entered and saw the floors descending from top to bottom with our current floor being the first. Jinx pressed the button for the bottom floor, the thirtieth, and we began our casual descent to hell.

Part Four

Chapter Thirty

Man

I had thousands of questions for Jinx spinning through my mind. When we finally reached the bottom floor, I expected us to be let out into some basement but the elevator doors opened to what looked like an ordinary corporate office. The sounds of phones ringing and papers being shuffled filled the stuffy, hot office air. Jinx scampered out of the elevator and I followed him down a grey, carpeted hallway.

"This is hell? Hell is an office?"

"This is just the thirtieth floor of Lucifer's tower."

As we passed through the office, we saw men and women in business attire going about their work. By the looks of them, you wouldn't think they were sentenced to torture for eternity.

"Who are all these people?"

"Hell's bureaucrats. Lots of souls live in hell, someone has to keep track of all their records."

"I guess they don't get to go home at five then huh?"

"No, they're doing paperwork until the end of time."

"What did they do to deserve this?"

"The employees in Lucifer's Tower were guilty of either having sinful imaginations or having seen something so traumatic their souls were deemed unacceptable for heaven."

"Evil imaginations?"

"Writers, artists, musicians, nihilists, none of these people committed sin but their minds were riddled with sinful thought."

"Is this where I'll be put to work for the rest of my soul's existence? I can't do it, Jinx. I've never been cut out for office work. I don't work well with others…water coolers give me anxiety. Please, don't let them take me."

"Calm down. We're only passing through. Lucifer will place you wherever he'd like and I'll bet it won't be here."

We took a right turn at a fork in the corridor and reached a mahogany door labeled with the number seven.

"Open it," Jinx instructed me.

I twisted the knob and it burned my palm. I was able to take enough pain to push the door open before pulling my hand back. A thin, wet layer of skin began peeling off the burn. Jinx entered the office and I went in after him. A giant desk rested in the center of the room where a short, shrewd man, *a Scrivener*, filled out papers he would pass to a roach. The roach would then crawl up a giant pile of paperwork that nearly reached the ceiling to place the paper at the top. Behind the desk was a giant window that gave me my first view of hell's landscape. Like a Martian inferno, the scorched red rocks of hell screamed with searing fire shooting up from the cracks. Jinx jumped up on the desk, on top of the scrivener's paper to grab his attention.

"Yes?" asked the scrivener.

"I have a soul to trade to Lucifer."

The scrivener opened up a drawer in his desk and found the proper paperwork to fill out. He hovered the tip of his pen over the blank spot that read 'Soul's Full Name.'

"What's his name?

"Benjamin P. Weiss."

The scrivener began writing, "Now yours?"

"Jinx the cat."

"Do you have a sample of the bartering object's blood?"

"Ben?" Jinx asked.

"Yeah?"

"Bend down."

I bent down toward Jinx and out of nowhere he scratched my face, leaving three slash-marks on my cheek. My blood and skin were left on the tips of his claw.

"Where do I sign?" Jinx asked.

The scrivener pointed to the line and in my blood, Jinx signed his name with his claw. The scrivener passed the form to his roach assistant to carry to the proper pile. Once my soul's destiny had been signed away, the scrivener stood up and walked over to the window. He pulled open the giant window, letting in a fierce wind that nearly blew him away.

"You have to jump," he shouted over the wind.

Our hairs blew in every direction until we forced our way to the window, against the wind.

"Don't be afraid," Jinx told me.

"I'm not..." I replied.

I jumped before Jinx and the hell wind grabbed me in its spiraling clutches, giving me a bird's eye view of hell entire. It was separated into cities, all connected by bridges, and sprouting from the center was a black creature reigning over them all. I assumed this was Lucifer. His giant wings were creating this wind every time they flapped. Suspended in the air, I wasn't sure what to expect, a gentle feather's landing or a smashingly painful plummet. Finally, the wheel of misfortune stopped spinning and decided my fate. The wind swung me directly, face first into one of the rock walls that lined the outer-crust rim of hell. Every bone in my body was shattered into thousands of pieces. My skull's sharp fragments lodged deep within my brain. I peeled off the rock wall and fell backwards in cartoonish fashion, plummeting down toward one of the cities of hell, completely destroyed.

Jinx gently landed on my blood-bloated stomach, bouncing off me onto the ground, totally unharmed. I spat up a gruel of blood and bones, passing out from the excruciating pain. Before I could even ponder my destruction, I was already being reconstructed. All my wounds and bones were healed for the sake that I suffer again until my dying lost its inherent humor. My eyes fluttered open to see Jinx above me.

"Where am I?"

"You landed in the city of Hush..."

"Hush?"

"They call it that because the people are too embarrassed to tell you their plight."

I sat up and looked around. The city's infrastructure was completely made of flesh, cracking and covered in festering warts. Even the ground below me, was a pink, hairy skin. The city's body was green and black in some patches, a deep red in others. I saw a number of people, wrapped in brown rags, gathered around a giant nipple pointing out of the ground as if it were some kind of hearth.

"What did they do to get here?"

"Carnal impulses. Lust. Irresponsible sex. Deviancy. Fetishism. Homosexuality."

I stood back onto my feet and walked over to the nipple so I could see what sort of citizens inhabited this city. I approached a sinner covered in rags that was turned away from me. Their hands were stretched out to the nipple as if trying to absorb its warmth. By their stature, I figured it was a woman.

"Hello?"

She turned around to reveal a hole where her nose should be. Her crusty, yellow eyes filled with terror and she stumbled back, trying to get away.

"Don't touch me. Get away."

"I don't mean you any harm, I just want to ask you about this place."

"Come any closer and you'll catch it too. Go. Get the hell away from us."

"You're saying I should be afraid of you?"

As she dragged herself back in retreat, her rags pulled up her thighs revealing a depraved and mutated flank of flesh hanging from her crotch. It reached down to her knees, this floppy piece of infected tissue. It was the essence of agony made sinew. I looked around at all the other souls and noticed similar mutations all around. Flaring bumps around the lips, men with masses the size of boulders in their pants.

Jinx walked up to my foot, shaking his head.

"They're all too ashamed to tell you they're sick."

"Is it herpes?"

"It's everything…you name it, AIDS, syphilis, gonorrhea, the list goes on."

From a distance, I could hear the faint but familiar sound of fingers chattering against the keys of a typewriter.

"Run," shouted the woman as she quickly got back to her feet and sprinted in the opposite direction the sound was coming from.

As the seconds passed, the sound developed in its depth and volume. It was too frantic to be finger-work. I looked out, searching for its source and saw what looked like brown paint flooding over the fleshy road from out the gaping vanishing point.

"Should we have taken her advice?" I asked Jinx.

I looked down to see my feline guide was missing. He booked it and was now a good hundred feet away.

"Fuck," I shouted then got up the nerve to run.

The more I ran, the more I realized I couldn't outrun this sound. It was enveloping all my senses as it closed in on me. It was so loud and disorienting it crisscrossed my other senses, sending the taste of shit into my mouth. I gagged a little and decided to look behind me to see what sort of death was approaching. It was a horde of pubic lice, so dense in their numbers, they appeared as one sea of brown. I turned back ahead, pushing myself past any mental of physical boundary to sprint for my soul. I'd exert myself to death before I'd let them devour me. Then, appearing in the distance, was a gross, erect phallus sticking out of the ground. So encrusted with disease-ridden skin it was, that it actually looked like Earthen rock sticking out of the flesh. I ran past the phallus and when I turned back to see the lice, I realized they had stopped to suckle upon its blood. I then heard Jinx calling.

"Don't stop. They'll drink it dry soon. You have to keep running."

I ran after Jinx until we reached a bridge that spanned across a sea of white, bubbling ooze. The ooze released such horrifying and noxious vapors, I had to hold my breath as I ran across, only pulling my hand off my mouth to vomit. Once Jinx and I finally made it to the other side, I knew we were now in a new city simply by observing the surface I was standing upon. The ground was a solidified brown sludge. I assumed I was standing in shit but when Jinx began licking at it, I figured my senses deceived me.

"What is it?" I asked.

"Taste it," he dared me.

I bent down and slid my finger on the surface. It was soft and warm. I looked into Jinx's eyes before tasting it to see if I was being tricked and realized he was totally serious. I shrugged before licking up the brown material and in moments, I smiled.

"Milk chocolate," I stated.

"My favorite kind," Jinx beamed.

"I suppose that ooze below the last bridge wasn't white chocolate, was it?"

"No. Certainly not," Jinx laughed. "It's a shame someone as funny as you will be doomed to such a fate." He wallowed then sighed.

"Where are we now?"

"Look around, take a guess."

I scanned this new city, realizing chocolate was but one of the confectionary materials used to build it. Ice cream, candy, and donut buildings littered the land, a waterfall of cola proudly sat in the glorious background.

"This must be where the gluttons go," I figured.

"No shit, Sherlock. It's called the city of Gurgle."

"So where is everybody?"

"Eating."

Jinx walked over to the window of a house made of waffles covered in strawberries and whipped cream. Inside was a single being so fat, he filled the entire house. His flesh pressed up against every wall, stretching and flexing the waffle interior.

"Does it have a face?" I asked.

"How else would it eat?"

We walked around the house to another window to see the body's face. It was covered in various bits of food, stuck to its skin by a layer of melted ice cream. I couldn't tell if it was male or female, even after seeing its massive breasts.

"I don't get it," I said.

"Don't get what?" Jinx asked.

"This is supposed to be punishment?"

"Just because they're not being torn to pieces or burned alive doesn't mean they're not suffering."

"Hell's nothing like what I've read."

"What have you read?"

"Dante's *Inferno*."

Jinx just laughed. "The reality of hell is far more depraved than what Dante could've ever imagined. He came from a time before evil truly had the chance to develop. How can you know evil before the holocaust, Soviet communism or Mao? What was the first thing you noticed about hell when that wind swept you over it?"

"I looked down and saw hell was comprised of cities, not circles."

"Exactly. Each of those cities is level to each other and equidistant from God. There are no hierarchies here."

"I still don't see how that's a punishment?"

"When you are told by your creator that your sins as a glutton are just as bad as that of a pedophile it is enough to make your existence hell. When a pedophile is told his crimes are no worse than a glutton's, how do you think it makes them feel?"

"Not too terrible, I'd imagine."

"Well, you're not a pedophile, so I suppose you wouldn't know it makes them feel rather inadequate."

Just then we heard the bursting of shattered glass. One of the windows around the back of the waffle house had ruptured open.

"What was that all about?" I asked Jinx.

"The poor fatty had to make room."

From out the broken window, the obese thing's puckered rectum protruded out and flared open. Like an explosion, a violent spray of feces shot out of its ass. Jinx ran up to the mound of fresh shit then after sniffing it, decided it was kosher to lick. I was about to puke before he turned to me.

"Don't give me that look, they shit chocolate...."

"So, I did eat shit?"

"Chocolate shit, yes."

This was going to be a long eternity. We kept walking down the streets of Gurgle until we came to a crossroads where Jinx turned to look and got so freaked out by what he saw he violently dashed up a marzipan light pole.

"Nope, not happening."

"What?" I asked.

He pointed down the street and I turned to look at what scared him so badly. It was a three-headed poodle puppy licking at a peanut butter cactus.

"You're telling me that the great Octavius, shadow of the saintly owl is afraid of a puppy?"

"Hey genius, if you didn't notice, that puppy has three fucking heads!"

"All the more to pet and nuzzle, *you scaredy cat*."

"If you're so brave why don't you go ahead and pet it?"

"Fine, I will."

Not for a second did I think it would bite my hand off when I strode over confidently and tried to glide it along its back. In one sheering bite, it snapped each of its three mouths and bit three different chunks out of my hand, disfiguring it into something grotesque. I screamed in terror.

"Told you." Jinx shook his head.

I ran toward Jinx, blood gushing out of my ravaged open wrist then with my legs straddled, I climbed up the same light pole Jinx was hiding atop of. I was able to hoist myself mere inches from the puppy's reach as it would jump and try to bite at my ass.

"Now look what you've done," Jinx shouted down at me.

"You shouldn't have dared me to do it."

"Well, I guess we're stuck here. That little monster isn't leaving until he eats us both."

"Dear God, help us."

Suddenly, the dog yelped and ran away as if stung by a bee.

Jinx quickly turned to me, his eyes twitching a bit.

"You idiot."

"What?"

"I forgot to tell you not to say that down here."

Green clouds began forming in the sky above. Rumbling, the punishment for my egregious error in verbiage was brewing deep within them. Once they covered the sky, a callous rain began to fall.

"Take cover," Jinx shouted as he slid down the pole.

I followed him back down and we both dove under a frosting awning. The rain fell all around us, melting everything with its toxic touch. Looking up, we noticed the rain beginning to burn holes in the awning. We knew we wouldn't have shelter for long.

"What now?"

"We're going to die, Ben. You for the second time and me for the first. I was really hoping I wouldn't have to die down here."

"So what? Won't we just come right back to life anyway?"

"No. You don't notice it at first but every time you die, you'll lose another part of yourself."

"You're saying part of me is already gone?"

"Your first death only removed a negligible portion of you it would seem. Hopefully this time you'll come back as the same Ben. You're making yourself less valuable to trade every time this happens, you know."

"Sorry."

"Sorry isn't going to cut it."

Suddenly, the awning collapsed and the acid rain showered onto us like liquid bullets, every bit of flesh in each drop's path would be disintegrated, from entry to exit point. We screamed in horrific pain until we were reduced to two smoking, unrecognizable puddles of ourselves. My soul trapped in my stew, each drop would hit me and splash me all around. What was once teeth, hair, cartilage, and skin was now one bubbling mess, rippling about. Finally, the sky's thirst for vengeance was quenched and the clouds parted above the city of Gurgle. In this moment of peace, the puddle of me began taking the shape of my body until becoming a Ben-shaped pool. Then as man once crawled out of the muck, I crawled out of myself, alive again.

"Ben?"

I turned around and saw Jinx was back to his old self too, looking a bit shaken as he sat beside me.

"Yes?"

"Good. You remember your name. What about Charlotte, do you remember her?"

"Who?" I hadn't the slightest idea who he was talking about.

"Oh dear, this is what I was afraid of…Charlotte was the love of your life. The reason you let yourself be taken here."

"I was in love?"

"Yes."

"Was she beautiful?"

"Yes."

"I wish I could remember."

I was indifferent. I had no idea what I had lost and until Jinx pointed it out, the fact I lost it.

Jinx sighed heavily. "Let's keep going, before I get any more upset."

We moved on together to the edge of the city where we crossed another bridge. Whatever substance flowed below each bridge would foreshadow the sin and city to come. Below this bridge happened to be a river of melted gold, shimmering in the flickering fire light.

"This must be where the greedy go."

"You're beginning to understand this place. It was engineered by a poet. Welcome to the city of Horrid."

What could possibly be more hellish to the rich after being made equal to all other sinners? What could possibly make them cringe at every glimpse of their surroundings? The streets of Horrid took on the landscape of a common ghetto. They were forced to live like the poor. All around there were only fast food chains to satisfy their hunger. There were no name brands to wear or European cars to drive. No beautiful women to exploit. I saw a sinner attempt to drag a massive anchor chained to his hands and feet.

"That thing is huge," I uttered in awe of the anchor's height.

"It's made of pure lead," Jinx replied. "For every dollar he earned, it must weigh another pound. You see what wealth would've afforded you in the afterlife? You were better off a starving artist."

"Seems as though neither fate is desirable."

"They might even be equal, all things considered."

We briskly moved from one end of the ghetto to the next, dodging stray bullets and stray dogs as they came our direction. Unlike the sinners in the other cities, those in Horrid didn't seem interested in talking to us. I got the sense even now, they considered me below them.

~ * ~

Beneath the bridge that lay ahead appeared to be a river of broken stones. As we crossed the bridge and got a closer look, we saw those stones had faces. Faces I had seen before in art history classes. They were all fallen gods and saints. Among them were the likes of Zeus, Horace, Thor and Jesus Christ. Seeing his face sent a shudder down my spine, for the statue seemed to be gazing back at me, pleading for me to reconsider a decision I didn't even know I made.

"Goddamn, would you look at that…" Jinx uttered.

Immediately, I became frightened, expecting certain death to come down from the skies again. Jinx saw me huddling for cover and began to laugh.

"I'm just messing with you. We can say that here and only here, in the city of Minus, home for heretics."

"What gives them that privilege?"

"Because it infuriates them a great deal to hear all their different gods get mixed up by the word. It's part of their punishment."

"Which is what exactly?"

"Let's find out what it is today, shall we?"

We strode into what appeared to be a town square, with walkways and structures made of stone. This was perhaps a replica of old Jerusalem, not that I'd know. The population had gathered at a stage and we took our places at the edge of the crowd. A man stood on stage beside a cylindrical drum filled with balls. He would crank the drum's lever and the balls inside would spin until the man felt some divine inspiration to stop. He opened a small door in the drum to retrieve one of the balls and opened the ball to read a thin strip of paper from inside it.

"Today you will all believe in a giant chicken that shoots lightning bolts from its eyes. Every egg you see will be worshipped as a demi-God. God is chicken and chicken is God."

"A chicken? A fucking chicken?" one Christian shouted in disbelief.

"We break the necks of chickens as a sacrifice to God. How am I supposed to worship a chicken?" cried a Jew.

"You know the punishment for heresy, guards take them to the stockades."

Two knights grabbed the dissenters and violently tore them away from the crowd, into custody. To the sound of glorious and heavenly trumpets, a chicken strutted onto the stage. It stood before the crowd, breasts puffed out and clucking out the voice of God. Like a wave, from the front to the back, the crowd kneeled down until reaching me. Too stupid to follow in the crowd's lead, I could feel the chicken glaring at me.

"On your knees, sinner! God is standing before you," demanded the man that anointed this chicken.

"Forgive me but as I kneel, I would like to ask God a question."

I knelt down before asking so as not to volunteer my head for the chopping block.

"Oh God, tell us, what is the meaning of life?"

The murmurs of a fearful public slithered through the crowd. They knew any question could get them all killed. 'Questioning God is violence against God' was the city's commandment. The chicken, though, had humility in its heart and so, it hopped from the stage, between the different heads in the crowd, all the way to me in the back. He looked into my eyes for a long minute. We both almost began to cry. In this moment, I was vulnerable enough to accept it as my savior. The chicken then jumped onto my raised knee to peck me in the forehead three symbolic times. This was his answer, perhaps trying to tell me the point of life was to suffer. I took this kernel of divine wisdom as undisputed personal truth.

"Thank you, God. Praise be to you."

The chicken then hopped away, back into its coop, marking the end of the procession. Once we were allowed back onto our feet, Jinx and I decided to keep moving onto the next city. Before leaving the square though, we saw one man, a Muslim, take a basket of eggs and throw them at his overlords.

"Allahu Akbar," shouted the Muslim, over and over.

He hurled about a dozen eggs at them, smearing holy yolk everywhere. The knights grabbed the Muslim and in front of everyone, took an axe to his head, chopping it off to mount on a pike.

~ * ~

The next bridge spanned over a lake of bodies, most of which were still alive, their limbs protruding out of the mass with weapons in hand to stab the body next to them. It was a war too concentrated to ever end, for in every pocket of this lake of bodies there was a soldier still consumed by dreams of victory. They would bite, they would stab, they would kick, punch and kill, forever in battle.

"This is where the violent go to suffer. From here on your job is to look up and walk behind me."

"Why?"

My eyes floated to the sky as arrows rained down upon the city. There were no archers firing them off, it seemed they spawned naturally, like tears from the sun. As Jinx led me forward, I kept my eyes on the skies to make sure we wouldn't get shot.

The city itself was one giant killing field and in any given direction you could see historic battles raging between enemy forces. The Union and the Confederates. The Nazis and the Allies. Shiite and Sunni. The Kuomintang and the Communists. It was as if history's greatest warlords had gotten their wish for war ad infinitum. However, without the hope for any victory, these wars became wasted efforts. You could see it in their faces as they slashed away and fired their rifles, they had become weary of the sight of blood.

"Landmine, up ahead."

Jinx side-stepped to avoid a mound in the dirt but as I glanced down from the sky to follow him, an arrow fell into my foot, splitting the boney structure in two.

"Fuck."

"What did I tell you? Always look upward."

"Well, at least I didn't step on the fucking landmine," I shouted, jumping up and down on one foot while holding the other.

As if Satan was testing me for his own entertainment, another arrow fell directly into the dirt mound and triggered the landmine to explode in my face. The front of my body was blown off and sprinkled all around the battlefield while the rear of my body fell backward like a hollow husk.

"Not again..." Jinx commiserated. "By the time I take you to Lucifer you'll be worth less than a sack of potatoes."

Like worms, every piece of my charred flesh crawled on their bellies back to the rest of my body to rebuild me. My guts jumped right back into their rightful cavities and when everything seemed back in place, my ashen black skin chipped off to reveal a healthy white beneath it.

"Ben, are you all right?"

"Who's Ben?" I asked.

"You. You're Ben."

"No, I'm not."

"Really? What's your name?"

I thought for a moment but in trying to recall, my mind seemed to run an error. Thinking this hard made me sick to my stomach and in one great upheaval, I vomited onto the ground. The puke seemed to be a living slush, my mind in liquid, seeping into the soil. Gone.

"You're almost totally lost. Poor thing. Oh well, onward, nameless soul. Don't you worry, the journey is almost over."

We kept moving until the next bridge appeared before us. The bridge led downward into the heart of hell and crested at such an incline. You couldn't see what was coming up ahead. I peered over the bridge's edge and saw nothing below but dead antimatter. The darkness seemed to stretch down for eternity.

"What's down there?" I asked Jinx.

"You think I'd know? Those that fall don't ever come back."

Jinx led me down the bridge until I could see the vile monster's spiked black fur back and abominable wings. With every flap of those wings, a pestilent wind would swell up around him, forcing him to cough up the bones of whomever he just swallowed. The further down the bridge we climbed, the more the beast's big belly would grow until it consumed the entire picture before me. Only a few feet away from the being's belly, a face seemed to burrow from inside its stomach to be born out of its belly button to speak with us.

"Do you have an appointment?" the face asked, glancing at me then Jinx.

"Yes, I'm here to trade this man's soul."

"One moment, please."

The face retreated back into the beast and seemed to squiggle up its body to confer with the beast's mind. Suddenly, leaning forward and down so he may come face to face with us, the beast nearly toppled over all of hell, dislodging rocks to come raining down all around us.

"Thank you for granting us audience with you, my Lord."

"You wish to trade me this man's soul?"

"Yes."

"What would you like in exchange for him?"

"Another soul."

"Whose?"

"That of my wife, who suffers here in the city of Hush where she was improperly sentenced."

"What do you suppose I should do with the raw material of her soul?"

"A woman on the human plane is pregnant with a male child. I want the soul of my wife to enter a rat's body that will look after that pregnant woman."

The beast thought for a moment, studying me.

"I agree to this trade." The beast crossed his arms and nodded to Jinx.

"He's all yours, Lord Lucifer."

"Excellent. Now leave us."

The beast stretched out his hand and opened up his palm in front of Jinx. Jinx stepped onto his hand and the beast lifted him back up to Lucifer's tower so he might make his way back to Earth. Jinx waved goodbye to me but I was too confused to wave back. Once Jinx was gone, the beast picked me up by the back of my neck and raised me up to his eyes for me to get a good look in them. His pupils glistened with entire worlds inside them. Worlds of possibility, of all things evil, the holocaust playing out in a sparkle in his eye.

"What is your name, human?"

"I don't know. What's yours?"

"Are you making fun of Lord Lucifer?"

"Should I have heard of you?"

"Yes. I am the morning star. I am the fallen angel. The master of darkness, creator of evil, and father of hell."

"You're not making any sense, either."

"You're human, are you not?" the beast asked me.

"What's that?"

"You are. Based on your body and your language, you must be human. If you're human, you must have heard the name Lucifer or Satan or Mephistopheles?"

"Can't say I have."

"Let me introduce myself to you then. I am your new master."

"Says who?"

"You are now in hell. My domain. Where sinners go to be punished for eternity."

"*So*...how do I know you're not a figment of my imagination, a hallucination or a character in a simulation?"

"I know your soul has been given to me but don't think I wouldn't prefer to swallow you whole right now."

"It makes no difference to me. This is meaningless. Who ever said you were big and scary? I think you're actually kind of cute for a being that doesn't exist."

"I don't exist?"

"Not to me. This place. You. God. None of it exists. I lost all my memory. I don't even remember my own name. So, if I don't exist, why should you?"

Suddenly, the beast grumbled with furious anger. His whole body trembled and with it, hell itself.

"How can you say Lord Lucifer doesn't exist? He stands right in front you. Feel my power!"

"Sorry, I don't know what to tell you. I wish I could be more impressed."

He roared with such intensity that hell began collapsing in on itself. The bridge that brought me here crumbled, sending the beast and I down into the abyss below. The cities too, all flushed away like water running down a drain. Finally, Lucifer's Tower above us came crashing straight down, stabbing into the beast's head, killing him. *Killing hell.* As we fell down the abyss, there was time for one last moment for feeling, thought, and being before everything ceased. No more hell, no more Satan, no more Jinx, no more me. It was pure nothing, death as it should be.

Epilogue

Woman

Getting pregnant made my mother decide putting me away in an asylum was a bad idea. We never saw Ben again after he visited me in the hospital and just assumed that he had split on us like my father had. It was eerie how much my life rhymed with my mother's. Ben's love was still an inspiration to me in everything I did, so I began reading more voraciously than ever before. Seeing as my pregnancy reaffirmed my clairvoyance, I read only two kinds of books, baby books and survival manuals. I learned how to build a fire, weapons, and shelter. How to survive the elements. What fruits, berries, and leaves I could eat. The first three months of the pregnancy went off without a hitch. I experienced the whole, healthy range of emotions and my body changed to incubate my son. I would name him Charlie, after Chaplin. I always considered him a living marionette. Another month passed and my world seemed totally at peace until the news plunged everything into total chaos. Trade wars between America and China escalated. First on cars, then electronics. Just about anything was taxed too high for anyone to buy. In turn, this suffocated our relationships with North Korea and Russia. The United States had already alienated most of its allies, so the time was ripe for a betrayal. I could sense it coming, probably at the hands of some European nation with a historic chip on their shoulders. I knew what was coming and I recognized the warning signs on TV.

One fine day, the wrong nation fired the wrong missiles in the wrong Arab territory. Suddenly, the world saw itself at the edge of calamity in an international conflict between the Russians and the Americans. No one was sure who was at fault or if it was all an elaborate set-up. The first bomb hit New Jersey. The second hit Los Angeles. The Russians memorialized Hiroshima in Newark and from out my Brooklyn window, I could see a mushroom cloud rising up from the catastrophe, reaching to heaven for help. Thousands were killed instantly, then the blast wave blew tens of thousands more away. Next, the shrapnel and debris flew as far as ten miles from the new ground zero, raining down upon New York like it was snowing metal death.

I knew leaving New York was my son's only hope but it seemed the rest of the city had the same idea. The streets were filled with panicked drivers, trying to frantically steer out of bumper-to-bumper traffic then careening into light poles. The news showed us side by side images of Newark and Los Angeles. The west coast had been devastated even worse. In a flash, the rich lost all power and authority. With downtown Los Angeles in rubble, the homeless and the mad seized control. Within a few hours, a knock came at our door as my mother and I sat in the living room, glued to the screen.

"Don't open it," my mother said before jumping off the couch and running into another room.

"Where are you going?" I asked.

"To get my gun," she said as she returned wielding a pistol.

Ready to fire at whoever could be waiting behind the door, my mother peered into the peephole to see who was on the other side.

"It's the cops."

"What do they want?"

"I don't know...there's three of them."

"All men?"

"Yes."

She fastened the door-chain then opened the door as far as it would go to speak with the police.

"How can I help you?"

"We're here to evacuate you from the building."

"What if we don't want to go?"

"Ma'am, we have reason to believe New York will be targeted next by these monsters. Do you want to be here when that happens?"

"Show me your proof."

"I'm NYPD...not CIA. I'm here to help. Now please, come with me."

"I don't trust you."

"If you don't open this door, we are prepared to kick it down."

"I'll shoot," she showed them her gun.

"We will too," the officer showed her his gun as the other policemen took a few steps back then charged the door with a brutal kick that snapped the wood off its hinges. My mother fired at the police and missed. They rushed in, slapped her hard across the face and sent the gun skidding across the floor before grabbing us both.

"Don't hurt my, daughter. She's pregnant."

"Quiet."

The cops pushed us out of the apartment. When we got onto the street, we realized the whole block was being evacuated and every neighbor came out of hiding into the street under the watchful eyes of the N.Y.P.D. At the corner of every block was a line of trucks. Each one had people piling into the cargo boxes like they were cattle or better yet, Jews being rounded onto a train. That's where all our minds jumped to first, this was the beginning of an American holocaust, an American fascism, based on economics, not eugenics. Destroying two major cities was a small sacrifice to bring about this epoch.

They separated the men, women, children and the sick into different lines. Without discretion, they pushed us ladies into the back of one of the trucks. My mother and I kept close to each other, not letting the hysteria of the crowd pull us apart. Her grip on my wrist left the impression of her hand, she held me so tightly. The police packed the truck to the brim with women then once they lowered the sliding cargo door, our screams converged into one desperate swell. We were left to chatter hysterically in the dark but I kept calm, reserving my energy and strength for whatever action might be required of me later.

Any suicidal or self-destructive tendencies that used to plague me were now wiped away from my heart and mind. What replaced those thoughts was a brilliant will to survive. This new found will, strength, and power all came from my child, who even in his unborn state, was channeling his nature into me. He was a warrior in the making.

"They're going to fucking kill us," one woman screamed.

"I told you. I told everyone. This guy was Hitler. We're being shipped to death camps," shouted another.

"Pray to God because we're going to need a miracle," a third continued.

"What the fuck will prayers do? God is what got us into this mess in the first place. We don't need to pray, we need to fight," they all became insane thus blind and defenseless.

My mother perched her chin on my shoulder and kissed me softly.

"Hang in there, Charlotte. We're going to be okay."

"I know, Mom. I'm not afraid."

"If something happens and we're separated, don't you worry about me. Keep your mind on you and your child. That's all that matters."

"I love you, Mom."

"I love you too, Charlotte."

I stayed silent and meditated. Reaching down into the depths of my soul, I could sense another consciousness within me, like discovering another world in there I couldn't penetrate but could rest my hand up against, like on the glass of a fish tank. Then my child's hand would touch the glass on the other side of my hand.

It felt like we were on the road for hours. Women began urinating and defecating where they sat, simply because they couldn't hold it in anymore. The truck began to wreak with an unspeakable stench. Some were certain they would die before we'd reach the destination, if the destination wasn't death itself. Others fell ill and began coughing incessantly. I could feel anger slowly simmering in me, I wanted to plug up their coughing pieholes with a fist so no harm could come to my very vulnerable baby. Instead, I kept faith my impenetrable mental solace was fortified enough that I was made immune to their illnesses.

Finally, after what had to have been at least six hours of driving, the truck stopped and we could hear the driver opening his door. A spell of silence fell over us as we waited to see what would happen. Three men in uniform, all armed with automatic rifles, pulled open the door to the truck and let a blinding daylight in.

"Everybody out. We're going to clean this shit hole while we refuel then you'll be right back on the road."

We piled out of the truck and stood around as the armed men watched over us, making sure not a single one would run. This was the middle of nowhere, a flat countryside with a dirt road and a single gas station with no one in sight, working or otherwise. First, a guard came around with a water hose to spray the back of the truck, cleaning out all our piss, poo, and vomit. At the moment that the driver began filling the tank with gasoline, one woman made a mad dash for an open field where there was no cover to obstruct the way of a bullet. Without a moment's hesitation or mercy, she was mowed down with a rapid stream of gunfire that separated her tops from her bottoms. Our entire tribe gasped. Some began sobbing uncontrollably, others fell to their knees, defeated.

"What was her name? Did anybody know her name?" one woman asked, screaming.

"She was my neighbor. Her name was Shelby Hollister," one woman mournfully wailed through tears.

My mother approached the armed guard that shot the woman dead and without any hesitation, slapped him across the face. The scene became so unnervingly silent the wind seemed to die. Every eye went dry to turn to her and the guard.

"What the fuck do you think you're doing, bitch?" he asked, his gun reflexively pulled up to her face.

"You cannot make me fear or respect you. If you shoot me, I will die showing these ladies that you're nothing but a pig."

The guard flushed red with total embarrassment. He was breathing so hard he could've combusted.

"What are you going to do tough guy?" my mother asked him.

"I should kill you right where you stand."

"You won't, because you're a coward…and you're afraid of what you've become."

"Shut up," he shouted my mother down, his rifle beginning to shake and stray off target from her face.

Another guard came over and casually put his hand on the barrel, lowering it to the ground.

"Stand down. I'll handle this."

"No, she's mine."

"I said, stand down or I'll have you thrown back to the dogs in central. Now take a walk and calm yourself the fuck down."

The guard walked away, punching the side of the truck as he went off alone.

"What is your name?" his superior asked my mother.

"Meredith."

"Meredith what?"

The superior raised his cellphone up to my mother's face and took video of her answer.

"Meredith Stein."

After getting her fake name, the guard stopped recording and put his phone away.

"Well, Meredith Stein, I'm going to put you on a special list. When we arrive at our next location, the guards there will make sure to give you special treatment that only special people on the special list get, understand?"

"Sure."

"Good...*Show's over now, ladies*. Get back in the fucking truck."

He waved us in and we all climbed back inside the cargo box. After the door was closed, it would be another six hours on the road for our scared and dying company. My hunger was only surpassed by my thirst and my thirst was only surpassed by my discipline. Some holy connective tissue was keeping all my organs stable as my baby stoically went on a hunger strike. At the end of that six hours, the truck stopped once again and this time when they opened the door, we weren't alone. Ours was one in a long line of trucks parked beside a tall barbed wire fence that seemed to run for miles. Beyond the fence was the sort of image all the students of European history among us would've foreseen, a sea of makeshift bunkers with white tent tops. Once we vacated the truck and were forced into a line, one of the guards approached my mother, holding up her picture to her face to identify her.

"Meredith Stein?"

"Nope," she answered. "You got the wrong girl."

"What is your name then?"

"Sally."

"Well, shit, Sally. The picture sure matches your face. What's in a name anyway?"

She kept quiet, staring at this smiling, toothpick-chomping sadist.

"You're coming with me, Sally."

The guard grabbed her by the arm and took her away from me. She didn't struggle or wish me goodbye. Without a whimper, tear, or so much as a curse against the men I was sure would be her killers, all I could do was simply mouth the words, "I love you." As if sensing I said my farewell, she turned and mouthed back, "I love you, too." She disappeared into the night and most certainly out of my life. I was supposed to cry. The moment was supposed to be a tragedy but I contorted it for my own means, changing its meaning into something I could use. My mother imbued me with her power and left with total faith I would survive.

The rest of us were absorbed into a longer line of all the ladies that were sent to this place. They came from every state in the North East, from Maryland to New York, to Maine, to New Jersey. We gossiped into believing this was going to be some kind of systematic killing of the poor. We agreed this was the rich making more room for themselves on the planet, so they could live without our incessant complaining. Once we filed into the camp, our portion of the line was taken to the side to stand to attention before a bitch in a black uniform.

"I am Commandant Mills. You ladies have been brought here for your own safety," the bitch began.

A sarcastic laugh bounced back at her, letting us feel free enough to begin mercilessly haranguing her bullshit before her very eyes.

"Yeah fucking right. You piece of shit."

"We know what we're here for, get it over with already, you murderers."

"You fat bitch. We see right through you."

"Shut up. You have nothing to fear. Fear will not be tolerated. I know this looks bad but you're better off here than on the outside. Out there you are dead meat. In here you'll be fed, clothed, given shelter, and washed. We have air conditioning, games, television. This is not a death or labor camp. Just because it triggers your pattern-based thinking, doesn't mean it is in fact history repeating itself. History is doomed never to repeat."

"Three women died on the way here. How were they kept safe?"

"That is unfortunate. We did not mean for anyone to get hurt. Whoever was in charge of your group was not following procedure. I will talk to you personally and get their information."

"Where are our children? My son is five years old and he was taken from me."

"They are safe and sound in an adjacent camp. You will be reunited with them shortly."

"When is shortly?"

"Don't get hysterical. We don't want to have to sedate you but as tensions are high, emotional responses become detrimental to group morale."

The bitch's body was speaking the language of authority. She had sucked our dissidence right out of us as she stood under the white, sniper tower lights that illuminated the camp. A woman at the far end of the line raised her hand. The bitch then pointed at her with her stubby, fascist finger.

"Yes?"

"Where are we?"

"Northern Vermont. You will receive all the details shortly, but first you will each be assigned a different bunker. If any women in the group are pregnant please step forward."

I made sure to freeze in place. A few fools followed her orders.

"Please follow my assistant to your special quarters."

The pregnant women followed another leather-bound lady on a walk I'd bet never ended. Meanwhile, we stood there stiff, trying to silently scream at them not to go.

"The rest of you follow me."

She led us down a long row of bunkers as far as the eye could see. After what seemed like ten minutes of walking, we arrived at our new home. Commandant Mills opened the door, flipped on a switch, and the rows of ceiling lights turned on one by one, illuminating the bunker. Two rows of twin-sized metal beds lined the walls, one row on each side.

"The first person in line take the first bed on the right, the second take the first bed on the left then keep alternating left to right as the line goes down. Go."

My bed was the fourth on the right side. I stood by it, stoically, as we all did.

"Who's hungry? Raise your hands," asked Commandant Mills.

I wasn't going to eat. I didn't trust these people with anything they intended for me to consume but still, so I wouldn't stick out, I raised my hands with the rest of the women. The one woman that didn't raise her hand was immediately confronted by Mills.

"You weren't fed along the way, how come you're not hungry?"

She struggled to answer knowing unprovoked and irrational punishment was always possible.

"I had a big breakfast."

"Big breakfast? Eggs?"

"Yes."

"Sausage?"

"Yes."

"Bacon?"

"Yes."

"Wowwweeee. Flapjacks too?" Commandant Mills asked, slapping up the woman's breast.

"A whole stack," she said, feeding off the Commandant's energy.

"Well, bitch, why the hell are you here with the rest of these girls? You're too fancy for them. Come with me, I'll take you to your hotel."

"No, please. I'm not fancy. I only have a few hundred dollars in my bank account," the woman begged.

"Bank account? Girl, you don't have a bank account anymore."

Commandant Mills gently put her hand on the woman's shoulder. "You're coming with me," Mills said then pinched the woman's shoulder so hard she yelped in pain. "The rest of you will have dinner brought to your beds in fifteen minutes. I've sampled it myself so you don't need to worry. It isn't gourmet but it's better than nothing," Mills finished.

Commandant Mills pushed the fancy woman forward to the door. Before leaving with her, Mills turned back to us.

"No one try anything funny. We have two armed guards outside and the eye in the sky is always watching…see you in fifteen."

Commandant Mills closed the door behind her and left us. Immediately, the girls either all started talking, crying or losing their minds. Meanwhile, as I had done this entire time, I kept to myself, relaxing on my bed and looking around the bunker, taking in my surroundings to see any weaknesses in design. There was only one door in and out of the barracks but that didn't mean it was the only portal to the outside. Suddenly, a girl screamed from the far down the bunker and we all turned to see what the trouble was.

"I can't take it. I can't take it. I hate rats. Get me out of here. Somebody get me out of here," the frightened lady shouted at the top of her lungs.

It appeared a rat scampered by her bed. So, logically, if there was a rat then there must be a hole. I casually got out of bed and slid down to the woman's side as others gathered around to console her. I pushed my way through them right up to her.

"Do you want to trade?" I asked.

"Trade what?"

"Bunks."

"You're not afraid of the rat?"

"No. I used to have one as a pet."

"Be my guest, it's all yours."

"My bed is fourth on the left. Can't miss it."

She ran over to my bed and I comfortably laid my head where hers had once been. I knew surveillance caught us make this trade but whatever suspicion it would draw was worth the risk if my hunch that the rat was my key to freedom was true.

Ten minutes later, as soon as Commandant Mills pushed open the door, the entire bunker went from a fearful chorus of doomsayers to a group of anxious mutes. Behind Commandant Mills was a long cart holding numerous plates of food, one for each of us. As soon as Mills reached the fourth bunk on the left where the rat-hating woman was resting, she stopped in her tracks, glaring at her.

"Aren't you supposed to be in the back? I remember your face. You were near the end of the line coming in."

"Oh, another girl traded bunks with me."

"Why would you agree?"

"There was a rat."

"There's a rat in here, all right. How about I assign you a bunker without rats?"

"No, please."

"Should've been happy with your own bed."

"I'm begging you."

"Stand up."

The woman stood up, crying her eyes out.

"Wait here until I finish giving out everyone's dinner."

Commandant Mills went down the line until we all got our food. She didn't give me a second glance, passing my bed. The dinner included a chicken drumstick, mashed potatoes, and a piece of cheese. What luck.

When Mills took the girl I had traded beds with to the door, she looked back one more time at us and with a booming voice proclaimed, "This is not the place to be bold, Charlotte."

As soon as Commandant Mills left, every woman began asking the one next to them if they were Charlotte. When one finally asked me, I told them no.

To make my overseers believe I ate their poison, I hid the chicken in one pocket and the cheese in another. The cheese would be my bait for this rat savior of mine. When more guards entered the bunker to collect the plates from every woman and saw that mine was eaten clean, they left me with a smile of approval. What I wouldn't give to see their faces tomorrow when they realize I'm missing.

~ * ~

Commandant Mills returned to the bunker for two final words before turning off the lights and leaving us in darkness. "Good night."

Because the Commandant expected silence, we were silent and because she expected us to stay put, I decided to run. I reached into my pocket, pulled out the cheese and placed it beneath my bed to bait the rat. After waiting about an hour in a false sleep, I began hearing the tapping of its tiny nails upon the floor as it hunted the bait with its nose. Once the rat finally snatched the cheese and ran, I went running after it, waking up a few girls in the chase. I made sure to follow far enough behind the rat I wouldn't scare it off course but close enough I could still see its shadowy figure apart from the darkness. By the end of the chase, I reached the far end of the bunker where the rat escaped beneath the last bed against the left-hand wall.

I looked down upon the girl slumbering above my way out and realized her sleep was deep enough I could get away with crawling under her bunk. I got on my belly then slid underneath it to feel around the wall until I found the vent the rat escaped to. It was screwed into the wall at each corner. I tried prying each tiny screw out with the tips of my fingers, nearly drawing blood from them but it was no use without a tool. I sighed, accepting failure and the sound that escaped my mouth traveled upward into the sleeping girl, making her roll around in her bunk. Startled, I jumped and my head shot up into some protruding object lodged in the bottom of the bunk's frame. The pain was excruciating. I had to bite my lip until it killed the need to scream. I touched my scalp and could feel the warm wetness of blood. I reached up at the protruding object that stabbed me and could feel its cold metal. I pulled at it, dislodging it from the bedframe and realized it was my salvation, a screwdriver. I could only assume someone left it there to readily open the vent for maintenance.

I quickly unscrewed the vent cover and upon removing it, I began to slither down the vent feet-first, forcing my baby to huddle closer to me than he had ever been before. I crawled down the ventilation system until seeing a light at its end. Once I reached the other end of the vent and saw the outside through the cover, I kicked it with both feet until breaking the cover off completely. Dragging myself out onto the dirt, I overcame the first obstacle of this escape. Next, I had to go unnoticed through a highly-surveilled perimeter and get past the fence.

I ran through the tiny crevices between each bunker, hopping between every pocket of darkness the moonlight wasn't touching. When I reached the main path out of the camp, I hid behind a wall, waiting for the search light and two working guards to pass to give me a blind spot to run in. Once I had been given that small window of opportunity, I made a mad dash for the fence. I knew it was too tall to climb and electrically charged, so I stopped only inches away from the chain-link. I looked up at the top, taking one big gulp.

"Hey."

I had been seen. I could feel myself turning white as they ran over. Before the guard could put me on the ground, a rat, the same one I imagine, ran between his boots and tripped him, face first, into the electrically-charged fence. Smoke rose off his body and neutralized the metal. Suddenly, sirens started blaring and several search lights fell upon me. I quickly climbed up his body to get a higher footing on the fence. I made it to the top and swung one leg over the barbed wire, deeply slashing into one thigh. I got the next leg over and slashed up the other thigh just as badly. Blood dripping to the ground below, I quickly climbed down and dropped off the fence. As soon as my feet touched the ground, I began sprinting as hard as I could into the night. The farther from the camp I got, the softer the sirens became until I saw a forest approaching in the distance. I ran into the heart of nature as it grew, multiplied, and festered in the evil night.

~ * ~

The first thing I needed was a weapon in case I was being tracked. I fashioned a tomahawk from a sturdy branch and a smooth sharp rock I found. Stripping a few vines to their sturdiest threads, I wrapped them around the rock and the stick to make this killing instrument whole. From there, I made a trap, digging a hole in the dirt that I covered with a bed of leaves. I set a few vegetables I roasted over a fire atop the trap and waited behind a nearby tree. The first prey I caught was a rat which I cooked and ate off the bone, to the bone.

The final test of the skills I had acquired in my survivalist readings was to build a shelter, a new home that would protect my child during his birth. I first hacked off enough leafy twigs that I could make a bed below a thick tree. I stood two long, thick branches at a forty-five-degree angle on either side of the bed and placed more branches, just as long and thick, across the two vertical ones I already set. I cross-hatched these branches into a roof, laying another bed of leaves over the roof and open sides of the shelter. This structure only lasted me a few days and, in that time, I began learning to mold mud into walls. I built a hut of sorts that would insulate heat and protect us from rain. It was in this shelter I gave birth to Charlie on a cold and star-filled night. My screams married the howls of wolves and though they could've easily come for me, I did not fear them. Ben's spirit was at my side, coaching me through the unfathomable pain of childbirth. As soon as Charlie made his first gasp for air, the campfire went out into smoke. He wielded such power.

About the Author

Robert Shepyer is a writer that blends the macabre and humorous in a way that will make you laugh so hard that you will squirt black milk out of your nose. With a tone that marries adult nightmares with children's cartoons, he tries to soften the suffering he sees in the world by translating it into a caricature of its worst self.

Bacchus Death Collective

Bacchus Death Collective is the story of a Bacchic death cult of Manhattan elites that are trying to shift the world's current Judeo-Christian value system into a Roman/Hellenistic value system based on the Roman god of wine and hedonism, Bacchus. The nine members of the collective are doomed to a specific death in order to fulfill a prophecy that will usher in the Bacchic age. The prophecy:

"One must die by fire, one must die by frost, one must die by poison, one must die by hanging, one must die by drowning, one must die by eating, one must die by being eaten, one must die by lust, one must die by suicide, one must survive and all must live in praise of Bacchus."

Chapter One

Number Nine's Necro-baptism
Number Seven – The Thief

"One must die by fire, one must die by frost, one must die by poison, one must die by hanging, one must die by drowning, one must die by eating, one must die by being eaten, one must die by lust, one must die by suicide, one must survive and all must live in praise of Bacchus."
Hersh, Number 1, Christ-Bacchus, God-child

How did I wind up here, behind this mask? I was wearing the same one that the rest of the boys were, it's face was that of a beautiful woman's with an ivy-sprig crown, blue eyes and a grinning, dragon-tooth smile. All the boys but Number Nine, the Musician, stood in a circle while the girls watched from the balcony. I looked up at Number Three, the Astrologer. She was speaking to her daughter, Number Eight, the Virgin, Number Ten, the Chef and Number Five, the Sommelier. Over the course of my travels, I learned to read lips, it would prove to be the one skill that made sure I'd get out of the temple alive.

"The full moon is in perigee. This only happens once every thirteen months," the Astrologer informed the Virgin, Chef, and Sommelier.

"They'll be driven mad..." the Chef added.

"As if they aren't already?" the Sommelier asked, rhetorically.

"The moon doesn't feed their lunacy. Their lunacy feeds the moon," the Astrologer finished.

Perhaps she was right, the temple drove Number Nine mad enough to take his own life. He had been a victim of his own tragic disposition, slitting his wrists that old-fashioned way. The boys had been waiting in a circle, shifting around in their uncomfortable dresses and masks, until finally Number Four, the Magician, dragged Number Nine's corpse into the center of the circle beside the ivory tub. The white tub was filled with deep red wine that suffused the temple with cigar-box vapors. The Magician lifted Number Nine up to the tub's lip to sit.

"May his dreams and memories be chained to this realm that they not follow him beyond. Take a good look at him, he is without his senses, and so his soul shall remain, unable to witness the glory."

The Magician paused and let go of Number Nine's corpse until it simply keeled over, to the side, splashing into the tub of wine. Once the body had been submerged, we all walked over to the tub's side.

"Each of you dunk him three times as tribute to Bacchus," the Magician commanded.

In order of our numbers, we lifted Number Nine up by his hair and dunked him back into the wine three times. I was the last in line to do so and once I had finished, it was my duty to lift the corpse out of the tub and onto the floor. I didn't think I could do it alone but when I tried, I felt superhuman power exuding out of every muscle. I looked at the moon, shining down from the oculus in the ceiling, it seeped a strengthening soma from out its craterous pores. With one arm, I took Number Nine out of the tub and threw him on the floor like a ragdoll.

The four women stood up from their balcony seats and walked down to the floor, knowing they would soon be needed for cleanup.

"In tribute to Number Nine's music, Number One will be playing the flute."

Number One, the Hierophant, Bacchus incarnate, lifted up his mask to reveal that thirteen-year-old baby-face we've all come to worship. The Hierophant was a special boy with a sad story. His name was Hersh and he was a hermaphrodite. Cast away by the world as a freak, he found a circle of people who would worship him as a God. He lifted his mask up to reveal those beautiful, golden blonde curls, his androgynous face, and those crusty lips. He brought his flute up to those crusty lips and played for us the perfect soundtrack to the violence that would ensue.

"In praise of Bacchus, tear the body to pieces," the Magician commanded again.

All of us spared no time in grabbing a limb or piece of tissue and pulling with all our might. Bones would dislodge and break before his flesh just split apart under the tension. Limbs, fingers, joints, and knuckles were flying up off the body in a frenzy.

"Embrace your divine madness. Let the nymphs seize you. The prince of pandemonium bequeaths you. Bacchus. Dionysus. The twice born. The lord of souls. Son of Zeus. Son of Semele. God of demonic silence and breathtaking violence. God of the most blessed ecstasy and enraptured love. Whose spirit is elemental to all that is created and destroyed and belonging to the Earth. In the name of this God, our God, who's come to us in human form, embrace your divine madness and tear this sacrifice apart," the Magician preached with startling theatricality.

When our hands were too slippery with Number Nine's blood, we resorted to our teeth and like jackals, ripped through the carrion without daring to swallow. With too many pieces to count strewn around the room, Number Nine had been divided up into an irrational number.

That's when the Astrologer and Sommelier pushed forward a vat of the mad honey. We all took handfuls of the honey to eat and celebrate the ritual's end. The Chef came around with a knife, stripping as much of Number Nine's fat off his pieces as she could collect. All the rest of him, the Astrologer, the Sommelier, the Virgin and the Chef would gather up to dunk in the mad honey for preservation.

We all lifted our masks and became men again.

"What now?" the Chemist asked.

"We drink," the Banker smiled and turned to Number Five, the Sommelier.

"I made a special wine for us tonight," the Sommelier informed us.

"Made it?" I asked.

"That's right, Jesus. Necro-baptisms and full moon perigees don't happen every night. This occasion was too momentous for just any bottle," the Sommelier replied.

With ample time between now and drinks, this is a good opportunity to make introductions. Hersh has to be Number One. Hersh is God as child, the homunculus, like Christ and Bacchus, he is twice born and from the water. Number Two is a man of just as much importance, a man of great vision but still, just a man. Number Two is the Banker, Charles Gaiman. Yes, *that* Charles Gaiman, of Gaiman-Billings, the mega bank. Stricken from birth with a terrible case of Omphalos syndrome, he is the financer of wars, governments, revolutions, political movements on the left and right, and cults like ours. Drunk with power and empowered to drink, at his old age, wine is his one true love, after his wife, Number Three. Opal Gaiman, Number Three, the Astrologer, is Charles' pregnant wife. Behind every great man, is a great woman and this great, big, gluttonous lady is responsible for the mad beliefs that infected Mr. Gaiman and led him to conduct this decadent experiment in the first place. The Gaimans' first child, Scarlet, is Number Eight, the Virgin. I've never seen a more beautiful blonde in my life, but I dare not act upon my impulses and touch her. Not to skip over too many heads, Number Four is the Magician, Salerno De Palma. With his giant, muscular frame, Sal is Hersh's greatest confidant. He would die for Hersh and our cult, because we are his key to the magical realm he's spent his whole life learning about. Mindy Oliver, perhaps my favorite of us all, is Number Five, the Sommelier or Somm, for short. She's a republican dyke with barrel-loads of attitude and has been working directly under Gaiman for at least a decade. Number Six is the Chemist,

John Rollins, a PhD paid to make our drugs. Then there's me, Number Seven, the Thief, a title I take no issue with. I came to this country illegally from Mexico to steal my freedom. I didn't come here to work, I came to here to explore, like Byron into Albania before the world had such rigid borders. I ventured through South and North America as a poet, my feet led by the ancestral memory of my grandfathers and a lyrical flow in my mind. I was on a quest to improve my potency for poetry. From the moment I stepped foot in America, I decided I would meet the man who owns this country and lo and behold, Mr. Gaiman found *me*. He took a deep affection and appreciation for my talents. As a skilled thief and lock-pick named Jesus Madrid, he saw the irony in including me in his collective. Number Nine was the Musician, Leroy Rich. Now, he's a bunch of honey coated pieces, stewing in the bitter goop. Number 10 Ten is the Chef, a transgender male to female. She was born Ingo Braun but reborn Inga. She hates us all, I'm sure of it. Why? Because we use honey for religious purposes and thus, get a pass to break our vow of veganism. That's us. That's Bacchus Death Collective. The BDC.

~ * ~

The boys were sitting around a table in the dining room. It's a beautifully decorated room with vines and ivy growing out of every crack and crevice and crawling up the legs of our marbled table. The only women allowed in our vicinity are first the Somm, to serve wine and second, the Chef, to serve dinner. The Somm approached first, carrying a bronze decanter that was sculpted into Hersh's face. She arrived at the table and introduced her wine.

"Tonight Bacchae, I made a special and ancient blend of what is known as a retsina. Modern wine cannot exceed a fourteen percent alcohol content but with this, the sky's the limit. It's more comparable to a tincture, really. I wanted to make sure we all forget about Number Nine as quickly and violently as possible. The base wine is a thick and tannic Saperavi vintage 2014, with grape resin. It was fermented by burial in the soil of a marani cellar in Georgia. The black plum smelling Saperavi's dry, peppery taste is complemented by blending in the mad honey and a pinch of sea water from the Mediterranean."

The Somm poured each of us a glass of the retsina. We all took a whiff and sip of the vulgarly stout drink. Many of us coughed out our severed taste buds. Hersh even gagged up a bit of vomit. After a few swigs, we discovered the delight in damaging ourselves.

"I taste sour cherry and black currant," the Chemist began.

"It's a warming wine," I continued.

"It's like sandpaper on my tongue, did you dip-in your rancid finger to stir this blend, you wretch?" the Banker asked the Somm, smacking his teasing crimson lips.

The Banker would always do this, offend the wine, torment the Somm, and silence the table. This was his show, no one but Hersh ever dared make a peep against him.

"No, sir. I used a metal stirrer and precise measurements. Do you not like it, sir?" the Somm asked with an undaunted discipline.

"Fetch me something I'm used to."

"I'll bring two bottles right away, sir," the Somm smiled and skittered off, away from the table.

In the awkward stillness that followed, the Banker just shook his head. "Can you fucking believe her?"

That's when Hersh hurled his retsina up all over the table. The Magician sprang up from his seat with a bowl and walked over to Hersh as if he was going to comfort the child. Instead, the Magician reached over and collected all Hersh's bilious red slop into his bowl.

"Mustn't lose a drop, sacred fluid...never know when I might need it for a ritual," the Magician then turned to Hersh. "Will you be spitting up anymore, Lord Bacchus?"

Hersh leaned over the bowl and spit out the debris lining his mouth before he waved the Magician away.

"Thank you, Lord Bacchus," the Magician said then returned to his seat.

The Somm returned with two bottles of wine for the Banker.

"What do we have here?" the Banker asked.

"Some Lubrusca from your own vineyard. 2001."

"Excellent, my favorite vintage. Grows just a few hours from here, up in the Fingerlakes."

"Interesting," I replied, feigning interest.

The Somm brought both bottles to the Banker and placed them before him.

"I won't be needing a glass," the Banker informed the Somm, who rolled her eyes at him. The Banker then continued, "What was that wine we baptized Number Nine in?"

"Standard Beaujolais. Something the Chef would cook with."

The Banker nodded then stood up from his seat.

"If you'd all excuse me, I'd like to drink my wine by myself."

The Banker then strode off, carrying both bottles of Gaiman Lubrusca.

www.ingramcontent.com/pod-product-compliance
Lightning Source LLC
Chambersburg PA
CBHW052000220626
47052CB00004B/1024